Saving Grace

Masters of the Prairie Winds Club
Book Two

by Avery Gale

Copyright © October 2015 by Avery Gale
ISBN 978-1-944472-19-1
All cover art and logo © Copyright 2015 by Avery Gale
All rights reserved.

The Masters of the Prairie Winds Club® and Avery Gale®
are registered trademarks

Cover Design by Jess Buffett
Published by Avery Gale

Thank you for respecting the hard work of this author.

This is a work of fiction. Names, places, characters and incidents either are the product of the author's imagination or are used fictitiously and any resemblance to any actual persons, living or dead, organizations, events or locales are entirely coincidental.

No part of this book may be reproduced, stored in a retrieval system, or transmitted by any means without the written permission of the author and publishing company.

WARNING: The unauthorized reproduction or distribution of this copyrighted work is illegal. Criminal copyright infringement, including infringement without monetary gain, is investigated by the FBI and is punishable by up to 5 years in federal prison and a fine of $250,000.

If you find any books being sold or shared illegally, please contact the author at avery.gale@ymail.com.

Dedication

For my cousin, David—whose advice when I first started writing continually reminds me to take a chance, because…"It isn't any of your business what other people think of you, so go for it. Do whatever you want to do."

Prologue

THE COOL, CRISP night air kissed Gracie's bare shoulders, setting off a wave of shivers as she stood on the sidewalk across the street from the small apartment building where she lived. She watched firefighters drag hoses into the run-down structure and thought back over the past twenty-four hours. How had her life managed to spin so totally out of control in such a short time? She wasn't sure she'd ever had a day quite like the one she'd just been through, but she was certain she wasn't up for another one anytime soon.

First the building superintendent for the dilapidated building she was facing had caught her as she was leaving for work to tell her that she was being evicted. He'd explained the entire apartment complex, including the ancient unit she lived in, had been sold and would be razed in less than six weeks. Her tiny apartment wasn't anything great by any stretch of the imagination, but the little second floor efficiency was the only thing keeping her from living in her damned car. And living in the piece of shit the DMV loosely referred to as a motor vehicle would quickly mean she'd be sleeping on a park bench since the automotive equivalent of the Titanic was sinking quickly. Hell, the last time she'd taken it in to the mechanic down the block from where she worked, he'd suggested euthanasia for road barge because it was on its last leg. *Smart ass.*

Gracie had moved to Austin ten years ago with her mother and younger brother, Alex. When her mom and Alex moved on to Dallas last year, a studio apartment in a dangerous neighborhood had been the only thing she'd been able to afford. And quite honestly, the idea of looking, *yet again,* for something in her price range was a daunting task to say the least. Hells bells and hopscotch, just the thought of it left her feeling both physically and emotionally drained.

Gracie usually walked to work, but the conversation with the super had burned up all of the time she'd allowed herself for walking, so she'd opted for the bus. Crap, the damned public transit behemoth that served her neighborhood wasn't much faster most days. And Gracie hated "wasting" the money to ride in the filthy bus when walking was free. Even though she had a car, she rarely used it because not only was it barely operational, but it had evidently been designed when gas was a dollar a gallon because the thirsty thing's fuel mileage was barely above the single digits.

Walking everywhere she needed to go was just one of the ways Gracie ordinarily tried to save money any way she could, because watching every penny helped ensure she could still afford to eat at the end of the month. One of the things she'd found she missed the most when her family moved was her mother's cooking expertise. Lovelle Santos always seemed to be able to create amazing meals from next to nothing. Gracie was convinced that particular gene must skip generations, because she'd certainly missed out. Even her brother, Alex, was a better cook and he couldn't even hear their mother's instructions.

Her younger brother had lost his hearing as a toddler and moving to the United States had been particularly challenging for him because reading lips in English was enormously difficult when it was your second language. When Gracie learned through friends that there were several kids in their neighborhood struggling with similar problems, she started volunteering at a nearby community center teaching a class to help Spanish speaking, hearing-impaired children and adults. Her goal had been simple and the work rewarding, she wanted to help them better adapt to their new English speaking environment.

After enduring the bus ride to work, she'd had walked through the front door of the small dress shop where she had been working for the past year and was met by the elderly owner's visibly distraught daughter. Learning that her sweet boss had passed away during the night had been a devastating blow. Gracie was heartbroken to learn she'd just lost a dear, wonderful friend and mentor, as well as her job. The family planned to close the shop by the end of the month, which meant Gracie had three weeks to find a new job *and* a new apartment. She'd finished out the workday in a fog of grief and disbelief before stumbling home in a virtual stupor.

As she'd neared the building where she lived, Gracie noticed a dark SUV sitting along the street. A new vehicle was so obviously out of place in her tired neighborhood that she had briefly wondered if it belonged to the asshat that had been pestering her friend and neighbor, Tobi Strobel. But, the SUV's windows were so darkly tinted Gracie couldn't see who was inside and in her exhaustion she'd let it go. Her hopes to chat with Tobi had been dashed when she discovered her bubbly friend wasn't home.

Gracie was keeping her fingers crossed that maybe…just maybe, her friend would be interested in looking for a place they could share since they were both about to become homeless. Hell, Tobi's employment situation wasn't much better than Gracie's, but at least she was still employed or had been the last time they'd discussed it. By the time she'd made her way upstairs and into her apartment after checking around quickly with neighbors to see if any had seen Tobi, Gracie had been too exhausted to even think about cooking. She'd opted to change into a pair of short shorts and a barely decent tank top before collapsing in a stupor diagonally across her daybed.

Gracie woke but her brain wasn't yet fully engaged enough to know what had awakened her, but the pounding on her door and the sirens approaching outside were enough to propel her into action. Before she was fully awake, she found herself standing on the sidewalk in the cool night air looking around at the shell-shocked expressions on the other residents' faces. No doubt they were also wondering if they'd have anything left when it was all said and done, even though they couldn't see any flames through the dense smoke. The group she'd been hovering with told her the fire had started in Tobi's apartment and Gracie had instinctively known it wasn't an accident. She'd started frantically searching all around the building and then when she hadn't been able to find her friend in the crowd, she'd gone into a panic.

When she'd found a young firefighter putting equipment back into one of the trucks, Gracie had badgered him until she'd actually begun to worry that he might summon one of the police officers on the scene to detain her. But he'd been understanding and kind as he had pulled her to the side and quietly assured her that they hadn't found anyone in the badly damaged apartment. She had sagged with relief and thanked him before quietly slipping around the building hoping to make her way back inside. Gracie had been trying to process everything that had happened when she noticed a tall, blonde god speaking to the building super in the narrow breezeway along the back of the building. Everything about him sent sparks racing up and then back down her spine until they felt like they were reaching out and touching every part of her. His face looked like it had been chiseled by some Renaissance master and his voice was so deep the vibrations of his words echoed straight to her sex.

But when Gracie realized Mr. Tall Blonde and Incredible was asking questions about Tobi and the fire in her apartment, she stormed up to stand directly in front of him. He towered over her but she didn't let that fact hold back the flood of pent-up emotion that resulted in a tongue-lashing he probably hadn't deserved. Every frustration she'd buried during her "Day from Hell" bubbled to the surface like molten lava and erupted like Mount Vesuvius.

She fired questions at him like a machine gun and crowded into his personal space until he'd finally wrapped his large hand around her wrist so she would stop shaking her finger at him. His crystal blue eyes had been almost dancing with mirth at her challenge and suddenly she was swamped by the realization he was even better looking up close. His skin was tanned and the soft wrinkles at the corners of his eyes and mouth gave her the impression of a man who smiled easily and often. His hair was a sandy sun-bleached blonde that was slightly shaggy and made him look like a bit of a rebel.

When she had finally paused to take a breath and her mind registered that he'd restrained her she'd felt a split second of fear race through her like lightning. But it had only taken her mind an instant to realize his expression held heat rather than anger, and her fear was replaced by a sense of longing that she couldn't begin to explain. She'd instinctively fallen silent and dropped her eyes.

MICAH HAD KNOWN immediately that the little spitfire currently shaking her finger at him was Tobi's friend the building super had mentioned. She'd battered him with questions without taking a breath until he'd started to wonder if she was ever going to run out of steam. Gracie Santos was obviously concerned about her friend and he admired her loyalty. But his instincts told him there was also something else going on with her as well. Her reaction was out of proportion to the conversation she'd overheard and he wondered what exactly had fueled her outburst. When she finally took a breath and realized he was holding her wrist loosely shackled in his hand, he'd seen a brief flicker of something too close to fear for his comfort move through her dark gray eyes. Before he could fully register the emotion and let go, it was gone and she lowered her eyes to the ground submissively. *Now isn't that interesting.*

He didn't release her wrist, and felt her heart rate accelerate under his fingertips as they pressed softly against her pulse point. "Look at me, Grace." Micah deliberately used the more formal version of her name to set himself apart from the other people in her life, deliberately trying to insure she remembered him. He studied her as she slowly raised her eyes to meet his. Her pupils seemed to dilate as he watched arousal banish the uncertainty in her expression. It was obvious the zing of electricity he'd felt when his calloused fingers had first brushed over her smooth skin had not been his imagination, nor did it appear to be one-sided. The tip of her pink tongue darted out to paint her rose-colored lips, making them shine even in the dimly lit hall. It had taken every bit of the control he had learned as a Dom to not push her against the wall in the small alcove behind where they stood and plunder her bow-shaped mouth. The short Daisy Duke shorts she was wearing displayed shapely, tanned legs he had no trouble imagining wrapped around his waist as she rode his rigid length. And her tank top was nearly transparent it was so worn. Obviously she had been reluctant to part with it, either it was comfortable or because she couldn't afford to. Either way, he was grateful because the view was a feast of pure visual sin.

She had listened quietly as he'd calmly explained that Tobi was fine. He'd also sworn to her that he and his friends planned to make sure she stayed that way. Since the fire had been quickly contained the damage had been limited to the living room, but the rest of the apartment had suffered a significant amount of smoke damage. Since the door was on the floor in pieces, there wasn't any way to secure the apartment, so he'd decided to salvage what little there was left. When he had explained that he'd be packing up her friend's belongings and taking them to her at Prairie Winds, she had volunteered to help. Micah had been grateful for her offer for several reasons. First of all, he was sure Gracie would be familiar with the lay out of the tiny apartment and would know where to find the most important items quickly. It would also give him a chance to ask her more about the man she had mentioned during her tirade who was causing problems for Tobi at work. But most importantly, it gave him a chance to spend more time with the tiny Latino beauty. And each passing moment had further convinced him that she might well be the woman he and his best friend, Jax McDonald, had dreamed of finding and sharing.

Micah sent Gracie into Tobi's bathroom to pack up anything she thought her friend might need for a few days stay at Prairie Winds. He had asked her to leave her phone with him so he could add updated contact information for Tobi and she'd readily complied. After Gracie had briefly explained about Tobi's co-worker, Micah had quickly called back to Prairie Winds to direct his security team to pick up Tobi's phone and disable the GPS location tracking. He had programmed his number into Gracie's phone and then quickly dialed his own phone so he'd have her number as well. He'd pointed out his number to her and asked her to call him if she had *any* questions or concerns.

Standing close, he'd said, "I'm worried that when Feldman realizes Tobi isn't here, he'll pressure you for information about her location." He noticed the almost imperceptible clenching of her jaw muscles. He lifted her chin forcing her to meet his gaze and asked, "Has he ever been a problem for you, Grace?" This time the fear flashing in her eyes was easy to read and he'd known immediately that she was already afraid of the man who had likely set tonight's blaze.

Even though Micah had always had a soft spot for "damsels in distress" there was something particularly powerful and unique about the vulnerability he sensed under the tough girl image Grace Santos tried so valiantly to show to the world—and it called to him. As they finished up the packing, he casually asked her about her day and was completely stunned when her eyes instantly filled with unshed tears. He sat down the box he'd been moving and quickly stepped in front of her and pulled her against his chest. He simply held her because he really hadn't known what else to do. "Pretty tough day, huh? The super told me that he'd let everyone know this morning the building has been sold."

"Well, yeah that started it. Then I found out my boss died and they are going to close the store where I work. And now the fire. Everything I own is going to stink, but it probably doesn't matter since I won't have a home in a few weeks. Now Tobi's gone and she was my only real friend." Micah hated hearing the desperation and vulnerability in her voice when she'd been all fire and sass just a few minutes earlier. There wasn't really anything he could do until he spoke with the Wests, so he just hugged her close, offering comfort in the only way he could. As a Dom, he understood the power of touch and particularly the importance of comfort after an adrenaline crash, and holding the lush little tigress against him was certainly no hardship.

After several minutes, he'd pulled back just enough to look down at her and sighed to himself at her slightly dazed expression. She didn't know it, but that vulnerability called to the Alpha male in him and sent fire racing up his spine as his Dominant side roared to the forefront. Micah quietly reminded Grace that she was to call him if she had *any* problems at all with Feldman or if she heard anything else that would be helpful in discovering who was responsible for the fire. As he'd driven away he'd had the sinking feeling that Tobi's friend was in danger, but he couldn't explain exactly why. Shaking it off, he looked in the rearview mirror and chuckled. He and the men he'd called to help him pack Tobi's apartment needed to deal with the amateur who was following them. And then he could focus on the fiery little beauty he'd hated walking away from.

Chapter One

Gracie had just emptied out the last of the boxes of sex toys that had been delivered yesterday and put the finishing touches on one of the displays for this evening's meet and greet event. Each of the small Forum Shops were ready for tonight's big opening gala and she found herself almost giddy with excitement. The addition the Wests had built on to the back of their BDSM club was enormous, but they'd divided it into "shops", which were more like mini-boutiques. They were arranged around a small courtyard that had been set up to resemble an open Roman rotunda.

Each shop was decorated to reflect the specialty items it featured for the various interests in what she'd recently learned was referred to as "the lifestyle." One shop was devoted to impact play and there were literally hundreds of items inside, all of them intended to be used in safe, sane, and consensual play. The light and wax shop offered a wide variety of colored and scented candles that melted at low temperatures. The laser wands had intrigued Gracie until she'd learned they were applied to a sub's "privates" and she'd dropped the device so quickly Tobi had burst out laughing. Nestled in among the shops was a small day spa that she and Tobi had given a test run yesterday. Gracie had been shocked at the intimate nature of the services they provided. She had been waxed, buffed, and polished until she'd giggled to Tobi that she felt like someone's high-priced Mercedes.

Every time she thought about it, Gracie still shook her head in wonder that her friend had married *two* men. But Tobi, Kent, and Kyle West all seemed happy, so she was happy for them. Gracie had seen the same affection in the interaction between Kent and Kyle's two fathers and their mother and wondered what it would be like to be loved that much…it was beyond her comprehension that she would ever find even one man that she trusted that much, let alone two.

Watching the West family was always great fun, their respect and love for each other was easy to see. They were gracious and accommodating, and Gracie had quickly felt like part of their close-knit group. But you didn't need to observe the ménage relationships for long to see that Kent and Kyle, along with their fathers, Dean and Dell, were Sexual Dominants. Watching the way the men interacted with Tobi and her mother-in-law, Lilly, always seemed to make Gracie's skin tingle and her pussy clench in need. Seeing the way Tobi responded to both of her men and recognizing her own body's response had made Gracie wonder if she wasn't a submissive also. Even though she wouldn't have ever believed it when she'd begun researching online after moving in to the small guest house at Prairie Winds, she'd read several descriptions of submissive traits that had resonated deep within her. She hadn't done as much research as she'd wanted to because she was usually so exhausted by the time she made it home each evening, she just ate a quick sandwich and went to bed.

After the fire in Tobi's apartment across the hall from her own small studio, Gracie had met Micah Drake, the head of security for The Masters of the Prairie Winds Club.

Thinking back on that night, there certainly hadn't been any question about the spark of electricity that had passed between them. Micah had programmed his number into her phone and told her to call if she had any problems with the man who had been harassing Tobi. And Gracie hadn't hesitated to call him a few nights later when she was being followed. She'd never returned to her apartment after that night.

Working as the assistant manager for The Forum Shops at the Prairie Winds Club was turning out to be a dream come true. After the Wests returned from their honeymoon it had been a full-on push to get the small shops finished, stocked, and the displays put together. All the advance notifications and marketing materials had been sent out to the club's growing membership list and the RSVPs had rolled in.

Gracie usually had to fight back her embarrassment when she opened a new box of merchandise. And helping set up displays featuring dildos and a variety of other "toys" often had her blushing so deeply that Tobi had often teased her about having hot flashes. She and Tobi had ended up on the floor in fits of giggles more than once as they'd tried to imagine what some of the items were used for. They'd made the mistake once of saying out loud that they were certain their imaginations were more creative than the truth, both having forgotten about all the high-tech security and surveillance equipment that surrounded them. Tobi assured her the next morning they'd been wrong…the truth had indeed been much more interesting than their imaginations. The sly wink Tobi had given her had spoken volumes and Gracie had felt a shiver of excitement race through her.

While Tobi, Kyle, and Kent West had been on their

honeymoon trip, Micah Drake and Jax McDonald had moved Gracie into the small guest cabin at the back of the Prairie Winds property. All three Wests had apologized because it was the smallest of their cabins, but in Gracie's opinion, the small cottage was absolutely perfect. The front porch ran the entire length of the one bedroom structure and had a comfortable patio set where she often relaxed with her morning coffee. The porch had numerous large potted plants and several of those seemed to be in continual bloom with vibrant colored flowers that made the porch a cheerful and comforting haven. The kitchenette was tiny but had everything Gracie could want including a microwave that actually heated up her food, something the tiny unit in her apartment had never done. The air conditioning and heat both worked and best of all, the hot water heater held enough hot water for her to wash her long hair *and* shower without being forced to either wait an hour or finish up with freezing water. It was clean and the furniture didn't smell like smoke. In her opinion, it was a vast improvement over the apartment she'd been forced to vacate.

Everything in the little guest house was modern and had been recently updated, and the only time it felt small was when Jax or Micah were there. Both men were big, but at six foot eleven, Jax made even the largest room seem small. Smiling to herself as she shelved the last items from another box of new merchandise, she heard the voices of men as they approached the shop she was working in. Gracie grabbed the empty cardboard box and made her way around the corner into the back room. The Wests had given numerous tours of the shops during the past month and she wanted the small space to look pristine when they entered.

Just as she was ready to round the corner to re-enter the shop she recognized a voice she had hoped she'd never hear again. The voice of a man who had promised her the sun and the moon, but had delivered his own particular version of hell on earth. The voice belonged to the man she had barely managed to escape years ago and she had no intention of giving him a second chance to imprison her. Backing slowly to the rear exit of the small shop, Gracie managed to open the door without making even a whisper of sound. As soon as she was outside she tried to calm her racing heart because fear wouldn't help her escape. When she felt a wave of dizziness move over her, she realized she was holding her breath and took in gulping breaths trying to push back the darkness that was edging into her vision.

Turning on her heel to make a run back to her small cabin to pack, Gracie ran directly into a rock solid chest. She felt a strangled scream leave her throat and her survival instincts kicked in as she struggled to escape. Just as the darkness returned, closing in around her, she heard Micah Drake's voice, "Grace? What the hell? *Stop!*" but it was too late, she had already fallen into the abyss of sweet oblivion and darkness swallowed her.

MICAH HAD BEEN on his way to the back door of the shop where he knew Grace was working to ask her to join him and Jax for dinner after the Opening Gala for the club's Forum Shops. He'd watched her open the door and slip out before letting the door close without a sound. The look of stark terror on her face had him rushing toward her. When she'd turned into his chest, he caught her in his arms to steady her, and the fear had quickly been replaced by out-

and-out panic. She'd gone completely wild in his arms and for a tiny woman, she was surprising strong. He'd used his Dom voice and commanded her to stop, but he honestly wasn't sure she had even heard him before she'd gone completely boneless in his arms.

He didn't know what had frightened her, but he knew better than to take her back into the small shop to find out. Scooping her up into his arms, he'd tapped his com unit and advised Jax to meet him at their cabin. He wasn't surprised to see his friend open the door just as he stepped onto the porch. "What happened? I could hear the concern in your voice and I was close." Smoothing Gracie's dark hair away from her face, he looked back up at Micah. "Is she alright? I'm thrilled she is here, but I'd rather she had walked in on her own." They moved into the living room and settled on the large leather sofa facing the fireplace.

"I don't know for sure what happened." Micah recounted the past few minutes and just as he finished, she started to stir. The instant Gracie's eyes started to flutter open, she was scrambling to get up. Micah recognized the behavior immediately and he knew from the way Jax's eyebrows had drawn together, he was thinking the same thing. People only operated in that fight or flight mode when they'd been up close and personal with life-threatening pain or fear. And even though Micah had every intention of finding out what the hell the little fireball had been through, his immediate concern was finding out what had triggered her reaction today.

Micah and Jax could both kill a man with their bare hands, and could restrain most men with one tied behind their back. However, restraining a terrified woman that you were trying desperately not to hurt was presenting them with a very real challenge. Micah finally managed to get her wrists manacled in his hand and used the same tone he'd used outside the shop. Again her reaction was immediate and this time Jax was looking at him knowingly with a raised eyebrow. Micah gave him a quick nod and returned his attention to Gracie. Sitting on the sofa next to her, he pulled her up onto his lap and turned her just enough that he'd be able to see each and every facial expression.

Jax sat close enough that he could pull her tiny feet into his lap. He placed his large hands over the top of her ankles in a gesture that was probably as much for his own comfort as it was for hers. Of the two of them, Jax was the more openly affectionate and it surprised most people because his size alone was so intimidating. Micah had asked him once why he hadn't opted to play professional football. Jax had just smiled and said hurting people for money had never interested him because he didn't really need it. Micah had assumed at the time his friend was saying that money didn't hold any real value for him, but he'd learned later the words had not been merely philosophical. Jax's parents were loaded. They owned an enormous conglomerate of energy companies and Micah still shook his head at the vast number and diversity of the companies under that umbrella.

Once Gracie had settled, Micah cupped her trembling chin with his fingers so her attention was focused solely on the two of them. "Grace, something has obviously frightened you. Tell us what happened." He had intentionally kept his words as statements rather than questions, because he didn't want her to feel like she had an out. Both he and Jax watched her eyes dart from side to side as if searching the room for some unseen danger and he could practically hear her mind reeling. "Grace? I gave you an order and I expect you to follow it. Do not try to edit your response, just tell us what happened." This time he'd laced his words with a bit more of the Dom-tone that natural submissives typically responded to without even being aware of the reason, and true to form, her words started tumbling out.

"I heard him. How did he find me? After all this time—I thought I was safe. But he was with the Wests and they...were so very close. How could he know? Please, you have to let me pack and leave here right away. You don't know what he can do. He has so much power and so much money. I'm not safe here. And none of you are safe with me here either." Nothing she was saying had made any sense to Micah, but her last words were just simply not true. Hell, the entire Prairie Winds property was a virtual fortress, including a well-stocked arsenal. The place was heavily armed and protected by six former Special Forces operatives who were living right on the property itself. *Not safe? Is she fucking kidding? Where in God's name does she think she can go that would be safer than where she is now?*

Chapter Two

JAX MCDONALD HAD listened to the craziness that rushed from Gracie in a torrent and smiled at the perplexed look on Micah's face. Micah was his best friend and had been for years. The man was as close to a brother as Jax had ever known. Micah Drake was absolutely brilliant when it involved security and computer surveillance, but interpersonal communication outside of a D/s scene often challenged him. Part of the reason he and Micah had decided to share subs was that their styles of Domination complimented one another's. They'd learned that the compatibility of their approaches had meant the submissive they were topping was well satisfied and consequently it meant they too were well satisfied. That wasn't to say their tastes in women were exactly alike, but they hadn't ever found it to be a problem. They'd used their ability to play off one another often enough that it had become almost routine, and this looked like it was going to be a perfect example of why they worked so well together.

Jax shifted slightly so he drew Gracie's attention just as he'd planned. "Gracie, I know *you* know who you are talking about, but Micah and I don't, so maybe you could start by telling us this guy's name." Jax knew full well that at six feet eleven inches tall, he intimidated most people. It had always amused him that for some odd reason he was usually able to overcome the problem with children and women fairly quickly. He'd always teased his teammates that it was because both groups could look into a person's soul faster than men, and he'd only been half kidding.

Gracie blinked up at him and then nodded quickly before responding, "Yes, I'm sorry, I wasn't thinking. Raphael Baldamino. Why is he here? He mustn't see me. You have to help me leave so I can hide. I can't go back to his estate in Costa Rica. Please." Her pleading voice and tears were Jax's undoing and he pulled her onto his lap and pressed her close to his chest and just held her trembling body against his own. As he cuddled her, Micah stood and moved quickly out the front door onto their small porch. Jax heard him speaking in low tones before the door had even finished closing.

"I don't know why he was here, *Cariña*, but I did see his name on the roster for this afternoon, but he was not on the list for this evening. So let's keep you right here until Micah can confirm that, how's that sound?" At her shaky nod, he went on, "I know Micah didn't get a chance to speak with you before everything went south today, but he was on his way to invite you to join us for dinner after the big opening tonight. But, since you are here now, let's see what we can do to set that plan in motion?"

As much as he wanted to keep her right where she was, he knew it was more important to distract that quick mind of hers. Given a few moments to worry, she'd start making noises about leaving again. He wasn't about to let her walk out the door until they had a handle on the situation and distraction was certainly better than arguing with the petite woman.

Gracie Santos had captured his heart when she all but fell out of her car and into his arms the first night he'd arrived at The Prairie Winds Club. He'd just stepped through the club's front doors when he'd been met by Kent and Kyle West and their submissive, Tobi. At their request, he'd turned on his heel and followed them right back outside. Jax had begun to worry when the Wests explained the woman Micah had been raving to him about for weeks was "incoming, status unknown."

Jax had barely managed to yank Tobi out of the path of Gracie's bucket of bolts when she'd misjudged the distance and speed of the vehicle racing toward her. Considering the condition of the car Gracie had been driving, he was impressed the thing had any brakes at all. He hadn't been surprised when she finally screeched to a halt directly over the spot Tobi had occupied mere seconds earlier. Once again he'd been grateful for his height and quick reflexes because the little hellion who married his two friends was fearless, reckless, and as Jax had learned quickly, she was also fiercely loyal and had a heart of pure gold. She'd won him over easily that first night and they'd become fast friends after everything had settled down.

Standing on that curb and catching Gracie Santos in his arms as she's clamored out of the damned clunker she'd been driving had been a game changing moment for him. Micah had been raving about the little Latino ball of fire but his descriptions hadn't really done the woman justice. She was petite by anybody's standards but next to him she was downright tiny. Her skin was a dark golden tan and had a dewy appearance that made it almost sparkle. Her waist length hair was like a wavy sheet of silk that reflected light like black glass.

Because of her injuries, the two of them had quickly discovered a mutual interest in American Sign Language since they both had younger siblings who were deaf. He'd immediately noted the deep bruising around her neck that had already started turning dark purple and he'd cringed when he realized her voice was almost inaudible. When club member Dr. Brian Bennett had asked him to step outside the small first aid station while he examined and treated her, the look on her face had stabbed straight to his heart. He'd offered to stay and she'd quickly nodded. His heart had soared until he registered her moan of pain at the movement. The trauma she'd suffered to her neck when Tobi's stalker had tried to choke her, had stolen her voice for almost a week. Later, he and Micah had moved her in to the guest cabin and she'd never had to return to that hellhole apartment she'd been living in. Dex and Ash had helped them pack up her meager belongings, and the four former SEALs had made short work of moving her to the Prairie Winds property.

Bringing his thoughts back to the moment, Jax rounded the corner into the kitchen and began setting out everything needed for their salads. He assigned her several tasks to keep her fear at bay. "You know, *Cariña*, we hadn't planned to make you work for your dinner, but I'm sure happy to have the help. I usually get stuck with all the peeling and chopping and it's just hell on my manicure." He shot her a teasing smile and was pleased to see his words had exactly the effect he'd hoped they would because her entire face lit up in a smile before a blush stole over her cheeks and she shook her head at his antics.

"I know what you are trying to do, Jax. And…well, I want you to know that I am grateful." She leaned over and gave him a quick hug and then went straight back to the job he'd given her. "And you know, I'm not much better at cooking than Tobi, so giving me the salads to put together was a very wise decision." When he clutched his chest and gasped in mock horror, she shook her head and laughed. "What else are you planning? Perhaps I can manage one more thing without summoning the local fire department. But in my defense, I want to remind you, the fire in our building didn't even start in my apartment. It started in Tobi's and she wasn't even home. Proof that you can just never out guess fate."

Jax looked over at her and smiled. *Truer words have never been spoken, sweet girl.*

MICAH WALKED BACK in and pulled Gracie into a hug. "Baby, are you alright?" When she nodded, he pulled back and studied her closely. He had been worried when he first opened the front door to find she and Jax missing, but he'd heard them chattering in the kitchen and let out a sigh of relief. "Well, Mr. Baldamino is on his way out the front gate. But he likely noticed a distinct change in the hospitality level after my phone call to Kyle. And I imagine that is going to pique his curiosity, so the more we know about him the easier it will be to anticipate his next move. To that end, while we're all putting dinner together, why don't you tell us what he did that sparks such a soul-numbing fear in your beautiful heart?"

Micah had been watching Grace Santos, worker extraordinaire, for the past several weeks and knew she seemed to think and process best when she was moving. He had literally documented hundreds of observations because learning everything about Grace had become his single-minded mission as soon as he had figured out how perfect she was for them. Micah had always studied anything that interested him with a focus that left his easy-going parents and siblings baffled, but he'd never been able to understand their "take life as it comes" attitude either, so it was all fair in his view.

While they worked together in seamless efficiency, Gracie shared how Baldamino had promised to send her brother to the best schools for the deaf that money could buy and provide for both he and her mother for the rest of their lives, if she would agree to live with him. Since she'd only been fifteen at the time, he'd also promised to let her finish her schooling and sworn there would be nothing sexual between them until after she was eighteen *and* had given her consent.

Micah and Jax looked at each other over her head with mirroring looks of disbelief. She had been staring at her hands and hadn't lifted her face but still must have sensed their reaction and known exactly what they'd done. "I know what you are thinking…how could she be so naïve? How could her mother be so dim? Why would anyone believe such a promise from a man everyone suspected had criminal connections? Believe me, we have asked ourselves those very questions a million times over. The simple fact is, when you have been financially ruined by political forces that don't even know you exist, and when the last time you ever saw your father and husband, he was being dragged out of your home in the middle of the night because he stood up for what was right and not what was politically correct…well, then you'll understand how easily poor decisions can be made."

Suddenly Micah felt like the slime beneath a slug. He'd never considered himself judgmental and the fact that he'd judged the woman he was already beginning to fall in love with frosted his ass. He turned to her and used his fingers to pull her chin up so he could look into her eyes. Hoping she would hear the sincerity of his words, he said, "We are both sorry, baby. And you are right, we did wonder. Part of our skepticism is from our years spent in the military. That experience has made blindly trusting anyone very, very difficult for us. And since we've never been in those circumstances, we have no idea how we would have reacted. I'm sorry we hurt your feelings. I'm sure you know we're both interested in getting to know you better." He stroked his fingers over the gentle curve of her high cheekbones enjoying the softness of her skin before continuing. "I can't promise you we won't make mistakes, but I can promise you we'll always own up to them. And neither of us will ever hurt you intentionally." Watching the acceptance of his apology flash in her eyes, he leaned forward and kissed her on the forehead before turning her to Jax.

"CARIÑA, I DO understand the desperation that goes with wanting the best for a loved one with special needs. And even though money was never an issue with my sister's education, finding someone that was worthy of our trust certainly was. There are a lot of wonderful people out there...just like you, that want to help. For us, it was a young woman named Jen Keating." Jax chuckled just thinking about Jen. She'd been hired as a companion and mentor for his sister, Elza, when she'd moved to college. But Jen had for all intents and purposes become a member of their family within just a few short weeks.

Damn, I need to text Elza and find out when Jen was supposed to return from Costa Rica. He'd known she was going there for an extended holiday, but hadn't heard whether or not she had returned. When he thought back on Gracie's comment about Baldamino's estate in Costa Rica, he made a mental note to contact Elza later this evening for more information. Something was stirring in his gut and he knew better than to ignore those his instincts.

Jax smiled at Gracie and shook his head, "There are some very benevolent people out there, but there are also some truly evil predators who will use every trick in the book to get what they want, even if it's a beautiful young girl." Jax watched as Micah ran his hand under her hair and he was happy to see some of the tension drain from her posture as Micah's strong hands massaged her nape. "There is a very real difference between someone who makes promises in order to gain control over another person and a Dom whose entire focus is on cherishing the submissive in their care. But we'll discuss that more in a bit. For now….I have a feeling we were just getting to the relevant part of your story when we interrupted you. *Cariña*, we need as much information as you can give us, so continue if you'd would please…"

Chapter Three

Gracie felt her whole body vibrate in response to Jax's last comment. There had been an unmistakable layer of steel command in his tone, she certainly hadn't missed, despite his attempt to shroud it with caring concern. During her many conversations with Tobi about what her friend referred to as "the lifestyle", Tobi had described that tone of voice perfectly. Gracie had heard both Kent and Kyle use what Tobi called their *Dom voice*, but what she hadn't been prepared for, was her reaction to it.

Not long after she'd moved to Prairie Winds, Tobi had loaned Gracie her e-reader, which had been loaded with erotic novels. Gracie had read each of the selections and many of them she'd read more than once. From the first story, she'd felt as if the author had been looking inside her own mind as they'd been writing. Everything she'd read indicated Tobi's earlier observation that Gracie was probably a sexual submissive also, had likely been correct. She'd had to be strong for so long, Gracie wasn't sure she could ever learn to let someone else take control, even for a few moments. She'd never done much dating because she'd never found a man who seemed capable of handling her strong personality and the need to be in control of her life. However, Tobi had assured her she'd met her match with the two men standing in front of her now.

During a late night margarita party several weeks ago, Gracie had reluctantly confirmed Tobi's suspicions when her friend had questioned whether or not she was interested in Micah and Jax. Once Gracie had finally admitted her interest in learning more about what she'd been reading, Tobi had literally been bouncing up and down in her seat. Gracie had laughed and threatened to tell Kent and Kyle how much they'd had to drink if Tobi didn't quiet down.

"Damn it, Tobi, quiet down. You know your men won't let their shirttails touch them until they rat me out to Micah and Jax. And what if they aren't really interested? Holy Mother of God, I'd die of humiliation."

Everything had changed now...in the time it had taken Raphael Baldamino to speak, Gracie's whole world had shifted. She'd felt it being tilted off its axis, and between one breath and another, she'd known everything she'd hoped for with Micah and Jax had been moved out of her grasp, and she mourned that lost opportunity. Looking up into Jax's face, she was surprised to see him watching her intently. Seeing that depth of focus and knowing he was studying her with the trained eyes of a highly skilled operative as well as a well-respected sexual Dominant sent a shiver up her spine she wasn't able to hold back. His expressions made her think he was seeing clear to the very foundation of her soul while waiting for her to continue.

When she tried to turn away, he put his hands around her waist and lifted her so she was sitting on the kitchen counter. He moved her knees apart and stepped up close. "No hiding, *Cariña*. Out with it so we can face it together. And don't think that I don't know about the books and your conversations with Tobi." At her startled expression he and Micah both laughed. "Sweet girl, this place is wired for sight and sound the likes of which would probably scare you if you knew the extent of it. Hell, I've been in military installations with less security. Everything in the public areas is fair game and many of the private areas are covered as well, for safety reasons. And that e-reader Tobi gave you works off our wireless connection so we know everything that has been downloaded onto it." He leaned closer and whispered against her ear sending another wave of lust-filled shivers through her. "Just so you know, we're thrilled that you are interested, *Cariña*. What happened today only solidifies why you should explore your desires, because taking care of his submissive is every Dom's number one priority. Let us take care of you, Gracie. Trust us to help you."

Gracie didn't understand her body's reaction to Jax, nor could she seem to control her mutinous arms when they reached out to him. He pulled her close and gave her a quick hug before stepping back. "Now, talk to us." Those simple words had her spilling the entire sordid tale. She told them about the months she'd spent locked in the suite of rooms in Baldamino's estate, how he'd chosen her clothing, her food, even what she was allowed to watch on television. Gracie explained there hadn't seemed to be any limit to his attention to even the smallest detail of her day-to-day life, but for the most part, he'd controlled everything from a distance. Toward the end of her time there, he'd come to her suite and sat on a small settee and chatted with her until it was time for her to go to bed. He'd insisted she change clothes in front of him, but he hadn't actually touched her until the week before her sixteenth birthday.

She had only been allowed to leave her suite when accompanied by one of his goons and even then, the path had to be pre-approved by Raphael. She hadn't been allowed in any open areas where she might have been seen by anyone looking over the perimeter walls. Raphael had insisted it was for her protection, but even as naïve as she'd been, Gracie had known that wasn't the real reason. Trips outside the estate's secured perimeter had been nonexistent.

By the time the three of them sat down to dinner she was battling the rolling in her stomach that always accompanied the revisiting of the memories from the time she spent as Raphael's hostage. Dredging up the memories of how terrified and desperate she'd felt during those long months, usually triggered nightmares that would take weeks to ease.

Her mind flashed back to the moment it had become clear he wasn't planning to wait for her consent *or* her eighteenth birthday. Even today she could vividly recall how she'd felt both relieved and panic-stricken. The thought of spending two more years in her gilded prison had depressed her, but discovering that he planned to "take her" on her sixteenth birthday, had sent ice through her veins.

Micah's voice cut through her rising panic, "Grace, we need you to stay with us, baby. How did you escape? Who helped you?" She could see the sincerity and concern in his eyes and she pulled herself together.

Pasting on a smile she was sure didn't reach her eyes, she continued, "Raphael sent me into town to the local doctor for birth control. The doctor was elderly and had been friends with my mother's father. He promised to stall a week on the shot and assured me he would have my mother and brother ready to go when I returned." This time she knew her smile was sincere, because the memory of how meticulous his plan had been still warmed her heart. He'd laid it all out for her in exacting detail so she wouldn't "fret." "When I worried for his safety he just laughed and said he was already dying and they had no power over him. He was so brave. True to his word, the next week I arrived at his office and was taken straight out the back door. My mother and brother were in the back of an old pickup covered with tarps and I crawled in with them. I was so relieved to see my family again and we huddled together as we were bounced in the truck making its way to the airport." It had been hot under that tarp and it had smelled putrid, but she'd been so exhilarated nothing mattered except being with her family again.

"We were on a plane to the United States within the hour. The doctor had gotten our travel documents and tickets. He'd even arranged for a woman to meet us at the airport in Dallas. She drove us to our new home in Austin and stayed for a couple of days to make sure we'd gotten settled in." Gracie felt herself sag in relief at having finally been able to tell someone what she'd been through. She'd told Tobi tiny bits of it, but she'd never shared it all with anyone before now.

"GRACE, HAVE YOU been able to share your story with anyone since you've been in the United States?" Micah was fairly certain he knew the answer to the question, but he wanted the confirmation. He'd watched her closely even as he'd mentally catalogued each fact she'd shared. Once she'd started, the story had seemed to tumble out so quickly it was as if she worried that if she paused she'd lose her nerve. He'd helped with various rescues as a SEAL and had seen other victims do the same thing. It was as if they had to purge themselves of the information quickly. And if they were interrupted, setting them on that path again was usually extremely difficult. Keeping herself and her family safe meant there would have been too much risk in sharing, but the price she'd paid had been enormous, and the cost had no doubt resulted in tremendous feelings of isolation.

"Not everything, no. It just wasn't safe, you know? I love Tobi like a sister—she is the best friend I've ever had, but you know how rash she can be. I didn't want her to get hurt by becoming involved or for her to get me hurt either." She tried to chuckle, but her effort had fallen far short. Micah pulled her hand to his lips and softly kissed the backs of her trembling fingers. He didn't say anything, he just gave her a few moments to pull herself together. "I've told her bits and pieces, but not everything." Glancing at the clock, Gracie cringed and then quietly said, "Please, I need to go back to my cabin and get ready for work. Tonight is a really important event and I don't want to let the Wests down. They have been so good to me and I really am very proud of what's been accomplished. I'll be happy to finish this later, but right now I need to get going." It was obvious that they had pushed her as far as they dared for the moment and both men knew it was time to back off.

It was evident to Micah that Gracie Santos was amazingly resilient, but even the most tempered steel could be bent if the heat was strong enough or the pressure great enough. He nor Jax would ever want to break her, but earning her trust was certainly going to involve crashing through more than one of the walls she'd erected around her heart. While he was certain the information she'd shared was truthful, he didn't, for a minute, believe she'd told them everything.

The more he learned about Gracie, the more he respected the little hellion buried deep inside of her. That Gracie had fire burning in her eyes as she'd shaken her finger in his face the first night he'd met her, but those same eyes were filled with fear and resignation now. The fear he had the power to change, but it was the resignation and sadness that seemed to bring all of his protective urges roaring to the surface.

Micah admitted a weakness for helping women in need, but comforting the damsels in distress had always been more Jax's forte. Micah could already see the deep affection and desire to shelter Gracie reflecting clearly in Jax's eyes. Micah's gut told him that things were going to get a lot more complicated before they evened out, and with Jax's focus centered on Gracie's personal needs, Micah was going to have to tamp down his own knight in shining armor feelings so he could focus on keeping her safe.

Micah knew he'd have to bring in the rest of the security team and he wasn't entirely sure how Gracie was going to react to that. Admittedly it was a given that there was always increased risk when more people were brought on board, but she was too important to gamble with her safety. Micah had trusted Ash Moore and Dex Raines with his life more times than he could count and he knew she'd be as safe with any member of his team as she'd be with either he or Jax. He'd speak with them quickly before tonight's events and then bring them fully up-to-speed at tomorrow's staff meeting.

Glancing at the clock, Micah was surprised to see how much time had passed and understood why she was concerned about getting back to her place. Jax set her on her feet and took her hand. "Come on, *Cariña*, I'll walk you to your cabin and wait while you change. Plus, one of us will be with you all evening, we'll rotate so it isn't obvious to everyone that we're standing guard."

As they passed him, Micah caught her wrist and pulled her back to face him, "Please don't leave an area without one of us accompanying you. Also, we'll be meeting with Kent and Kyle first thing in the morning." Micah pressed a quick kiss to her lips before sending her off with Jax. Heading toward the Forum Shops, he fell into step with Ash and Dex.

As they walked the short distance, Micah updated the two former Navy SEALs and saw their reactions to the information reflected in their body language, despite the fact their facial expressions hadn't given away a thing. Stopping at the edge of the courtyard, he turned to them, "I don't think I have to tell you that this is personal for both Jax and I. We haven't made any secret out of our interest in Gracie and this doesn't change that."

When both men nodded, he returned the gesture and turned to walk away. Dex's voice stopped him, "Micah?" When he turned, both men were looking at him intently. Dex's words were short, but powerful, "We've got this." Micah nodded in acknowledgment and smiled to himself as he entered the courtyard and headed toward where the Wests were standing. He'd appreciated Dex's reassurance. Just hearing the words let him take a deep breath for the first time since Gracie had shared her story. He knew her safety was in some of the most capable hands in the entire world—he just prayed it would be enough.

Chapter Four

Tobi West leaned back against a glass display case and took in all the activity surrounding her. She'd been watching things unfold during the entire evening and she couldn't help but wonder what the hell was going on. It had only taken her a few minutes after entering The Forum Shops to know something was definitely up. Her husbands were both acting like cats dancing on a hot tin roof. She didn't know why they seemed to be suddenly "on alert" but she'd noticed a change in them after their late afternoon meeting with some Costa Rican playboy. Before they'd given him a tour of Prairie Winds they'd been totally relaxed and jazzed about the Grand Opening.

There were several more people working security than they'd originally scheduled and neither Kent nor Kyle had left her side since they'd come downstairs from their living quarters above the club. Hell, they'd even followed her to the restroom. Tobi could see that her friend, Gracie, was beyond flustered, even though most people would probably never notice the small tells that indicated how truly "rattled" the ultra-efficient woman was. But she and Gracie had been friends for a couple of years now, and those subtle changes were easy for Tobi to spot.

Each time she'd ask Kent or Kyle what was up, they'd all but patted her on top of the head and told her not to worry. *Yeah, like that's gonna be effective. Sometimes having two Doms for husbands is a serious pain in my ass. Treat me like I'm a dim-witted three year old...that just frosts my fanny.* If there was one thing she didn't tolerate well, it was being treated like an incompetent child. *Maybe it's time to pull out the big guns.* Scanning the crowded space, Tobi looked for Lilly. Her mother-in-law was quickly proving to be her biggest ally and staunchest supporter, and Tobi had no qualms at all about recruiting her. When she spotted her *secret weapon* on the other side of the courtyard she was mid-stride when a sharp swat on her ass brought her to a dead stop. Kyle pulled her back against his chest and wrapped his arm around her in a move that was clearly meant to anchor her close, and darn if it didn't send a flood of moisture to her mutinous pussy. His arm pressed her breasts up until Tobi was worried they might actually pop out of the corset top she was wearing. He leaned down and spoke right against her ear using a voice that was pure sin set to sound.

"Where do you think you are going, kitten?" *Drown me, he knows that turns my knees to jelly and makes me wet.* He also knew she was completely bare under the short skirt she was wearing since he'd been the one to relieve her of the new panties she'd bought for this evening's opening. He had turned her over his knee and spanked her soundly for wearing them too. Although the orgasm he'd given her hadn't done much for ensuring the spanking could actually be viewed as a punishment.

"I was going to speak with your mother." Even she could hear the breathlessness in her voice, so there wasn't a chance in heaven *or* hell that he'd miss it.

"Kitten, don't think I don't know you're going there to enlist her help. You've already ask both Kent and I several questions about what's going on, so let me save you the effort, love. Our mom is not 'in the loop' as you say, and we've already promised to tell you everything later. So, for right now, I suggest you keep your lovely pink ass right here or I'm going to give a little impromptu demonstration on all the ways to discipline a bratty sub outdoors." Her breath caught and she heard him chuckle. The louse was playing with her. Well, two could play that game. She subtly rubbed her tender ass in a slow figure eight against the hard length of his cock, pressing back just enough to elicit a hiss from him. When she smiled sweetly over her shoulder at him he grasped her chin and caressed her bottom lip with the pad of his thumb. His smile was suddenly much more sinister looking and his words were almost growled.

"Oh lovely wife of mine, you are playing with fire." If she couldn't go gossip with Lilly, she fully intended to use up a whole box of matches. Oh she knew there would be consequences, but that was part of the fun.

Turning her head even further so she could give him her most seductive look, she winked and let her inner Mae West bubble right to the top. "Count on it, big boy." The look on his face was absolutely priceless and she'd have given anything to have a picture of the moment. The only other time she'd seen him speechless was the day they'd met in the middle of a highway during one of the worst thunderstorms Tobi could remember. She'd been standing on the centerline of the blacktopped road after her car had been pushed into the rain-flooded ditch by a passing truck. No one had been willing to stop as she'd stood along the road's edge, so she'd taken a stand where she knew drivers couldn't ignore her.

When he'd barely missed her and finally come to a screeching halt, she'd charged him like a small but mighty steam engine. He'd been shocked speechless until a crash of lightning that was much too close for comfort jarred him back to his usual Dom self. She'd teased him more than once that if it hadn't been for that damned lightning, she'd be his Domme now…and oh how sweet the punishment always was for those remarks.

Tobi had been so lost in her thoughts, she hadn't even realized Kyle had been moving her until she found herself up against a tree along the edge of the walkway. They were on the backside of the large oak so they weren't immediately visible to their guests, but they certainly weren't hidden either. Tobi felt the familiar spike in her heart rate and her breathing started coming so fast she was almost panting.

"Big boy? Really, kitten? You thought that was an appropriate way to address your Dom during a club event?" His tone had gone to the pure icy-hot Dom tone that always set her entire body on fire, and even though she'd seen a flicker of a smile pass through his expression, her anticipation still sent a rush of moisture to flood her sex. Glancing around, Tobi looked for Kent, hoping he might be willing to play Sir Lancelot and come to her rescue.

"And if you are looking for your other Master to pull your sassy ass out of the fray, you can give that idea up. He has gone to ask one of our dads to escort your ally and frequent partner-in-crime into one of the shops." *Oh shit.* She really was in trouble if they were making sure Lilly didn't know what they were up to.

"WELL, KITTEN, I'D say judging by that curse word you just muttered you realize you really are in hot water. We've been very lenient with you—obviously too lenient. We do own a BDSM club and you should be setting a good example when we are in public, not behaving like a brat. Did you realize that another sub and one of our most respected Doms not only witnessed you grinding your ass into my cock, but they also heard your flippant remark?"

Kyle wasn't about to tell her the two people he'd mentioned were both Club employees and that she'd actually been setup. Earlier this week they had heard Tobi mention to Gracie that he and Kent had been so busy recently they hadn't played with her in "forever." He and Kent had both been stunned, standing stock-still glaring at the monitor and shaking their heads in disbelief. The one piece of advice all three of their parents had given them when they'd married Tobi, had been to guard against becoming so wrapped up in *creating* their lives that they forgot to *live*. And less than a month after returning from their honeymoon they'd done exactly that.

"No sir." Tobi was actually starting to worry now, she already knew that the only time they had really and truly punished her was when she'd made them and herself look bad in front of other club members. When she saw Kent striding back toward them, carrying his club bag, she actually heard herself whimper. She knew that damned bag was full of torture devices of all shapes and sizes. Some of them were just downright devious, and her Masters knew how to use each and every one. Tobi was really starting to panic and the black dots that always plagued her when she was frightened started waltzing at the edges of her vision.

KENT WALKED UP just in time to see Tobi starting to sway. He'd seen her pass out more than once from holding her damned breath when she was frightened, but so far, they hadn't figured out how to help her break the habit. He wasn't sure what Kyle had been saying to her, but his damned brother should have been facing their playful little sub because the blood had completely drained from her lovely heart-shaped face. Whatever Kyle had whispered against her ear had terrified her and that wasn't at all what this was supposed to be about. Kent reached up and pinched both of her nipples right through her dress. "Sweetness, take a breath. *Right now.*" His barked instruction got the attention of almost everyone around them as well as Tobi's. Suppressing a smiled, he noted that at least she had gulped in a huge breath of air. When she blinked up at him as if she were trying to get her eyes to focus, he let his smile surface. Looking down at her, he said, "I don't know what we're going to do about you holding your breath when you are afraid, but we need to figure it out—soon."

Kyle spun her around so quickly that Kent had to steady her. "What the hell? Kitten, are you alright?" Kent glared at his brother, but let it go when he saw the guilt in his eyes.

Kent gave her a solid swat and grinned when she yelped. He knew it had to have stung after the spanking she'd gotten before the party and that was perfect as far as he was concerned. "She's fine—for now. But I do believe our little subbie has earned herself a punishment for her saucy attitude." He moved so he and Kyle were shoulder to shoulder and gave her a slow perusal. He let his gaze move purposely over her entire body—so she'd feel it as if he'd actually touched her. He had to bite back his grin when she shuddered. "Are you wet, sweetness?" He had deliberately settled his eyes on her skirt.

"Y...yes, Sir." Now *that* was the tone he liked to hear, a nice level of uncertainty, but no real fear. This was the place they liked to work from. Her apprehension would feed her arousal and that was exactly what their little sub needed. As they'd pushed her boundaries, they'd discovered Tobi enjoyed a wide variety of scenes, but childhood physical and emotional abuse had left her with some very real triggers. They wanted to help her overcome them, but this wasn't the time or place. The biggest hurdle they faced was her abject fear of them being truly angry at her. She almost always panicked and held her breath when she thought they were genuinely cross with her. He and Kyle had actually considered speaking with Dan Deal about the situation. Dan was a personal friend and a practicing psychologist in Austin. And as a Dom at Prairie Winds, he'd have a unique understanding of their situation. Kent made a mental note to give him a call next week.

Kent slowly raised his eyes back to her face. He had to hold back his smile when her nipples drew into tight little buds under his gaze. She was so incredibly beautiful and deliciously responsive. They'd searched for the perfect woman to share for years and just when they'd given up finding her, Kyle finds her standing in the middle of a fucking highway in the rain. *Unbelievable*. But right now, their lovely wife needed some attention from her Doms and they were more than happy to comply.

Chapter Five

MICAH LED GRACIE outside the small shop for a break after Regi offered to fill in for a few minutes. Regi was Prairie Winds whirlwind administrative assistant. They all joked that she was the one who really kept the club running, she was a pixie with an Amazon attitude. She'd been with Kyle and Kent since before they'd even opened the doors and Regi had become a "little sister" of sorts to all of the staff. Micah had taken one of Gracie's small hands and Jax clutched the other as they moved away from the crowd gathering at the far end of the sidewalk.

"What's happening up there? Hold up a minute. There wasn't anything on the schedule for the courtyard." Micah hid his smile at her inquiry and curious expression.

When Gracie pulled her hands from theirs, turning to start marching up the cobblestone path toward the group, Micah shackled her wrist with his hand and pulled her back. When he smiled down at her she frowned at him, and he nearly growled as the Dom in him started to push forward. Reining himself in, he slowly leaned forward and kissed the furrows between her brows. "Baby, if you were our sub—that frown would have just earned you a few swats—and you'd be getting them right here, right now." He grinned when her eyes widened and her pupils dilated despite the fire dancing in her eyes at his words. He slid his palm under her hair and grasped her nape to tilt her head back to ensure that all of her attention was focused solely on him. There was a lot of sass in her, but he didn't think she was ready for them to tackle that full on just yet. He hoped she'd never be completely "tamed" because he was coming to love the challenge that was Gracie Santos. "As you know, Tobi has been feeling a bit neglected by her Masters lately." Micah bit back a smile as Grace nodded slowly even though she was obviously mulling over exactly how anyone else knew what her friend had shared in confidence. "And instead of talking to them about it, she spoke with you. So her Masters are reminding their sweet subbie that she belongs to them, and that includes her worries and fears, right along with every delectable inch of her body."

Micah knew Gracie's curiosity had finally won out when she asked, "How did you know that? That was confidential information. I don't want her to think I betrayed her." She bit her lower lip and he wanted to pull it away with his own teeth and then crush his lips to hers, instead he cupped her chin and pried it loose with his thumb. Tracing over her full lower lip with the calloused pad of his thumb, he simply watched her for several seconds. Her words might have been spirited, but her body language was all but shouting her vulnerability.

"Baby, we weren't kidding when we said this place is wired for sight and sound. Remember, you are dealing with former Special Forces operatives. And we were damned good at our jobs—because, to be honest, you're either good or you are dead. I've seen some of the best die because somebody else didn't do their job." Micah had done Grace's background check before the Wests hired her. When he discovered that she had aced her citizenship test, he knew how hard she must have studied. Anyone who cared enough to study that hard would appreciate the freedoms soldiers fought for each and every day. Micah had also noticed the softness in her eyes whenever one of them mentioned soldiers, and that tugged at his heart. She clearly had a deep respect for her adopted nation and that upped his respect for her exponentially.

He'd been briefed earlier that day on the scene Kent and Kyle had planned for Tobi. He and Jax had agreed they would keep Gracie away from the action until they knew more about her needs and interests. Letting her walk up on a scene would be tantamount to taking her into the club without interviewing her first, and that simply didn't happen at Prairie Winds. All club members were personally screened by Micah and then interviewed by either Kent or Kyle, and usually both. The system they'd established before the club even opened was time consuming to be sure, but it had done wonders for ensuring the safety and confidentiality of their membership. The *only* exception had been Tobi.

Micah had purposely placed himself between Gracie and the action she'd been trying so hard to get a look at. And with Jax pressing against her back, Micah felt certain Gracie had all but forgotten her worry about what was happening behind him. "Tell us about your interest in the lifestyle, baby." He purposely gave her a few seconds to wrap her mind around his question because he knew he'd surprised her. "Since we already know you've been reading about it, we're wondering, do you see yourself in any of the stories you've read?"

He knew by her reaction that he'd nailed it, but he waited for her response. Her adorable expressive face played her emotions as clearly as if she was speaking them aloud. *Hope you never play poker with anyone but us, sweet girl.*

Even though the men at Prairie Winds played cards for money, they'd always made the subs play strip poker. Their card shark group had all laughed at Regi and Tobi's outrage when they'd been the only ones naked.

Gracie's restlessness brought him back to the moment and he regretted having lost his focus. She needed and *deserved* his complete attention. He'd be willing to bet her mind was spinning at the speed of light. She was probably trying to figure out how he knew that she was seeing herself in the submissive characters featured in the novels she'd been reading for the past few weeks.

Over the years he'd talked to numerous subs who had confided that they'd started reading erotic romances when they'd realized something was missing in their relationships. Most of those had explained how utterly shocked they'd been to discover how much they had in common with the submissives in the stories. Most of men *and* women had sworn they would never have seen themselves as sexually submissive before reading the novels. Most had shaken their heads as if they could still barely understand how it had happened, but once they'd opened themselves up to the experience it was clear the D/s dynamic was exactly what they'd been missing.

Gracie had been averting his gaze as she fought an inner battle, he placed his hands on both sides of her head and sighed inwardly at the feel of her silken tresses sliding along his fingers. The image of those waves of black silk sliding over his bare thighs as she took his cock deep into her throat flashed through his mind and his entire body responded with an almost painful lurch of desire. When she brought her dark eyes to his, he softened his expression and was reassured when she relaxed into his touch. "Grace, there is no right or wrong answer. Don't overthink your responses, baby. When a Dom asks you a question you only need to answer it immediately and honestly. Aside from that, you will not be judged or punished for your answers. Punishment comes from behavior, not honesty."

The change in her was immediate and truly remarkable. Her eyes cleared and she met his gaze straight on. His words had clearly empowered her and he couldn't have been more pleased—until he heard her words. "Yes, it's true. But I can't do it."

He knew immediately what she meant, but he was going to force her to explain herself anyway. If things were going to progress like he and Jax hoped they would, then clear lines of communication needed to be established and kept open at every turn. "Explain what you mean, please." When she seemed to stiffen, he added, "The key to any successful D/s relationship is communication, baby. And in a ménage it is even more critical."

Jax leaned down and spoke against the delicate shell of her ear, "*Cariña*, my position behind you is both literal and figurative. Master Micah and I will always have your back, love." Micah knew his friend had used the term Master intentionally just as he had when referring to Kent and Kyle with Tobi. They needed to ensure she remained as close to a submissive mind-set as they could get her so her answers would continue to be as unguarded as possible. Jax had told Micah earlier that he wanted Gracie to begin acknowledging them as her Masters and the shift in her eyes showed his efforts had not been in vain.

"I have to stay in control or I fear I'll find myself locked back in that gilded prison. He'll use my mother and brother as leverage. And even though it is going to break my heart, I'll have to stay away from them from now on." Micah watched the tears flow unchecked down her tan cheeks, but he didn't move to wipe them away. The terrified woman hiding behind the bravado needed this opportunity to vent the emotions, and he wouldn't stand in her way. He and Jax waited quietly as she took a couple of steadying breaths and then simply leaned against him.

Micah knew he was a hard man to surprise—years of missions in and around the worst this world had to offer had left him skeptical on his best days and often he was downright cynical. But with that simple gesture of trust, Gracie Santos had completely stunned him.

Wrapping his arms around her, he didn't do anything but hold her for long seconds. When he felt her shoulders shaking as sobs racked her tiny body, he looked up at Jax and with a quick nod toward their cabin, he knew his friend would understand his unspoken instruction. Reluctantly he pulled back and used his thumbs to wipe away her tears. "Baby, you feel perfect in my arms and I'm asking you to please put your worry aside for tonight. Now, I want you to go with Master Jax. I'll join you in a bit. Everyone is heading for the exit and things here are winding down quickly so we'll be able to finish this up in short order." He was grateful the opening hadn't been scheduled for a regular club night or he'd have been stuck working, and tonight she needed both he and Jax.

Micah watched as Jax scooped up the woman who had just knocked the world right out from under him and cuddled her into his massive chest. His friend's long strides took them out of Micah's view in mere seconds and he had to shake himself to clear his thoughts. Looking to the side, he noticed Dean West standing to his left smiling.

"It's an incredible rush isn't it?" Micah still felt like a deer in the headlights and knew it probably showed in his expression. A knowing smile played over Kent and Kyle's dad's lips. "When you find the right woman and accept that she is yours. There isn't anything like it, son. But I'm warning you, don't blink…because just as the song says, it goes by faster than you think and you don't want to miss a minute of it." Kyle and Kent's parents had all but adopted each and every one of their sons' fellow soldiers, and now they'd added the other members of club's staff to their brood as well. When Micah smiled, Dean nodded and said, "Now, let's get these stragglers headed toward the exit so we can both get back to our women. I don't know who's chasing that sweet, little gal, but we'll take care of it—don't you worry." Micah didn't question how the man knew, he just nodded and they both went to work.

Chapter Six

KENT CARRIED HIS exhausted wife toward the back door that led to their private elevator. He couldn't wait to get her inside their apartment. She had played into their hands so perfectly this evening it was almost as if the entire scene had been scripted in advance. It hadn't. And he'd been jolted, once again, at the pure perfection of the woman he and his brother had been blessed with. Watching her beautiful ass push back for more swats had made him so hard he'd nearly embarrassed himself in front of everyone watching. They hadn't really intended to draw such a crowd, but having an audience had so clearly fueled Tobi's desire that it had been more than worth the extra effort it had taken to play it out as a full scene.

He and Kyle had both given her five swats even though it had only taken the first two warm ups to get her head right where they wanted her. Kent had never seen a sub who could slide so easily into a submissive state of mind as their sweet wife. Tobi had worked herself to the bone since they'd returned from their honeymoon and tonight's opening had been a smashing success as a result. They'd made sure her spanking was entirely erotic because it really had been meant as a reward despite what they'd told her.

Holding her in his arms as she pressed her soft face against his chest was one of the sweetest feelings in the world. "You are so perfect, sweetness. Every reaction, every response, every whimper, soft sigh and moan...each of those belongs to your Masters and you showed that in bursting color and surround sound tonight. You made us very proud, love. And you're going to be rewarded for that."

She snuggled higher in his hold so her lips were pressed against the side of his neck and when she inhaled against his skin, he felt his knees weaken. *Christ, the woman completely undoes me. She holds my entire world in her delicate hands.* He'd sent thousands of requests out to the Universe over the years asking that *their* woman be sent onto the small stage of their lives. He'd sent most of those requests heavenward during long nights under the stars in some godforsaken location and then he'd prayed they hadn't missed her.

Knowing she'd needed them these past weeks and hadn't felt secure or confident enough to tell them had humbled him. Clearly he and Kyle had a lot to learn about being effective Doms in a long-term relationship. But they needed her cooperation as well, so there was a "come to Jesus" meeting in her near future. But tonight wasn't going to be about that. He felt her soft, warm lips move in a breathy whisper over his neck as she spoke, "You smell so good...like light and love..."

Kent hadn't thought he could love her any more, but he'd been wrong. As he strode into their large bathroom and settled her on the cool marble he smiled down into her brilliant green eyes. He hoped like hell Kyle hurried up or his resolve to wait until they were all three together was going to crumble like sandstone. He moved her legs apart and stepped into the open space. Leaning down, he pressed his lips against hers in a kiss that went from sweet to scorching in the time it took him to slip his tongue through her sweet lips.

Angling her face and slipping his hand over her nape, he deepened the connection and let the reminder of how much they needed one another move over them both. Her lips were satin smooth, warm, and as sweet as honey. Tobi always seemed to plunge into a kiss as if she were trying to pour every bit of herself into the melding of mouths. He'd ask her about it once and she'd simply shrugged, "It's my soul's way of speaking directly to yours. And I want to make sure what's being said is clear." The simplicity of her words had rocked him to his very foundation and he'd instinctively known that she'd handed him a very important piece of information. He'd even written it down and put it in a small frame on his desk because it was a piece of the legend on the map to her heart.

Kissing Tobi was the sweetest thing in the world and Kent didn't intend to waste a single moment of his time outside of his head so he refocused his attention on the dance their tongues we currently engaged in. Kent hadn't planned for the kiss to morph from a sexy rumba into a tortured tango, but his control where Tobi was concerned was always tenuous at best. Feeling her dueling with him for control ignited something in him and his entire body responded. Pulling her hands from where they clenched his shirt, he pinned them behind her back and felt her arch into him, pressing her breasts into his chest as a moan rumbled in her throat.

Kent hadn't even realized how lost they had both been in the moment until he heard a soft chuckle from the door. He reluctantly pulled back and gasped for air as he leaned forward and pressed his forehead against hers before kissing the tip of her nose and then turning to his brother. "Well, I think it's a good thing I took the dads up on their offer to finish up outside. I'm not sure how long you could have held out against our lovely woman's charms, brother." *And isn't that the God's honest truth? She owns both of our souls.*

Kent looked intently into her eyes and hoped the depth of his love showed through. "True enough. Let's get her naked and nicely pliable before we fuck her into oblivion, shall we?" He felt more than saw the subtle shudder that moved through her. *Perfect.* Tobi was the most responsive woman he'd ever met. Not long after she'd agreed to explore the lifestyle, they'd done various scenes in their efforts to determine what worked best with her and they'd been thrilled to discover she responded equally to touch, visual, and verbal stimulation. The little minx also loved a good spanking, so they were constantly searching for something creative to use as punishment. Their only challenge had been her absolute fear of them being angry with her.

"Sounds perfect. I'll just watch as you undress our lovely sub, because the view so far has been fucking hot." Kyle might have been speaking to him, but his eyes had never left Tobi, and Kent watched her eyes dilate until only a small ring of green surrounded her enormous pupils. He could hear her respiration speed up and the pink blush over her heart was spreading rapidly. Reaching around her, he kept his movements slow and deliberate. Pulling down the zipper on the back of her dress so she could feel each tooth as it released, he vowed that her next dress would be a halter because he loved untying the knot and letting the softness of silk fall like waves of water, revealing the sweet treasure beneath.

"Kitten, you please us more than you know. Your submission and trust is the greatest gift we've ever been given." Kyle wasn't as close as Kent, but he couldn't miss the unshed tears that filled her pretty eyes. Kent hated the fact Tobi was so unaccustomed to compliments. They'd noticed that about her early on and had been working to build her self-esteem, but they obviously still had a long way to go. The personal losses she'd suffered hadn't broken her, but they'd shaped her to be sure. Kent had wished a thousand times that she could see herself through their eyes, if only for a moment. It would only take a glimpse for her to know how perfect she was.

"I almost ran you know…not because I was scared…but when I thought I'd embarrassed you again? I just wanted to hide." Her whispered words surprised him and flicking a glance to his brother in the mirror, Kent knew Kyle was equally dumbfounded. Was she really *so* frightened of them that she'd actually considered running? Had they been too hard on her? Questions flooded Kent's mind. She obviously noted their astonished expressions because she took a quick breath and went on. "I know I'm not a perfect sub," when he'd started to protest she'd carefully pressed her warm fingers to his lips to still him. "No. Please let me finish." She took a deep breath and then continued, "I'm not a perfect sub and I probably won't ever be. But pleasing you and being able to see that you are proud of me…well, those are the things that drive me to keep trying."

When she stopped speaking, they just waited while she tried to pull her control back into place. "I love pushing myself until I feel like I've mastered everything I attempt. I won't argue that and I don't want to discount that it is just a part of who I am. But seeing *your* pride in me, fills a part of my heart that I could never fill alone. Does that make sense?" She waited just a couple of beats before continuing, obviously her question had been rhetorical, even though Kent knew both he and Kyle would have loved to have answered her. "Besides, these shoes wouldn't have let me run very fast and the idea of tripping over my own feet and sprawling out over the courtyard with my bare ass exposed didn't seem like a very good plan at the time. But now that I think about it, that's exactly how I ended up anyway, so perhaps I should have given it a go." The cheeky grin that slowly crossed her face told him she'd deliberately changed directions and they'd allow it...for now.

Kent tried to hold back his laughter but failed miserably. "God, you are so fucking perfect."

"Well, she would be if she was naked. Now hurry up or I'm going to take over." Kyle's voice sounded rough, but Kent saw the smile on his brother's face and shook his head at the empty threat. They had the rest of the night to remind their lovely wife of all the reasons—good and some not so good—she should never be tempted to run from them.

Chapter Seven

RAPHAEL BALDAMINO STUDIED the digital images he'd received earlier this evening. The ethereal beauty of her face was even more compelling now than it had been in her youth. There was a luminescence about her that he'd never seen in anyone before or since. She was the only woman he'd ever craved with a desperation that shredded every ounce of his control, and seeing her standing in the courtyard he'd been in only hours earlier set off a rolling wave of possessiveness in his stomach. Rose was sandwiched between two men whose expressions were easy to read and the white-hot flames of jealousy in his heart were making his chest ache. Both men's faces clearly showed their desire for what was his and that knowledge was burning like acid deep in Raphael's gut. He'd never shared well. And he certainly didn't plan to start now. Rose had escaped him once, but she wouldn't again.

He'd been directed to The Prairie Winds Club by mutual friends when he'd mentioned an interest in starting a club of his own on the *Osa Peninsula*. Raphael loved living in Costa Rica, even though it seemed on occasion a bit too removed from most of his business interests, the atmosphere and the view made any inconveniences well worth the hardship. And he hadn't ever really given up his hope of finding Rose. He had, however, incorrectly assumed she'd valued her Central American heritage enough to stay closer to home. *Another lesson I'll be teaching her soon enough. She will learn quickly I'm sure. I can see the light of intelligence still dances in her beautiful eyes.*

His tour of the Wests' club had been going well and he'd been particularly interested in the elaborate metalwork they'd had specially made. Even though their club's western themes wouldn't be suitable for what he was planning, Kyle and Kent West had assured him that EGA Fabrication would be able to create exactly what he had in mind. They'd planned to give him the contact information, but after Kyle answered a call everything had changed. Whatever the caller said had obviously troubled him and totally derailed the connection they'd been building. The tour had quickly ended and he'd been unceremoniously escorted to his vehicle.

The sudden change in his host's demeanor had set off alarms for Raphael, so he'd quickly called in a few favors and secured one of the highly coveted invitations for the exclusive grand opening of the Forum Shops for one of his business associates. Micro-technology had meant the club's strict no cell phones or recording equipment ban was easily circumvented and the pictures he was looking at had wirelessly arrived within seconds…and they were perfect.

Raphael wasn't sure what had prompted his contact to zero in on Rose, but the man had earned a substantial bonus for his insight. Perhaps it had been the protective stances of the men who appeared to be sheltering her—whether from seeing something or not being seen, Raphael wasn't sure and he really didn't care. In one of the shots the wind was stirring her hair and the silken strands appeared to be dancing on the breeze. Her eyes were focused on something out of the frame and the intensity of her gaze made her look almost regal. Tracing his finger over the large print in his hand, Raphael outlined her angular jaw and high cheekbones. She had always reminded him of a Peruvian Princess who'd been mistakenly born into poverty a half a continent north of where she belonged.

Shaking off his wayward thoughts, he wondered…had she seen him today and been frightened? God knew she had reason enough to fear him, because there would most certainly be consequences for running away. The elderly doctor who had helped her had paid with his life. Later, when Raphael learned the man had already known he was dying, he'd been furious that he really hadn't denied the bastard anything.

Raphael would begin searching for Rose's mother and brother immediately because he knew they would hold the key to controlling the beautiful flower that would eventually belong to him. Just holding her photograph in his hands had his cock responding with a thundering hard-on that was pressing painfully against his zipper. He'd need to find a woman to relieve that ache after his plane landed in San Jose. There would be a helicopter waiting to take him to the estate, but the pilot was well paid and would willingly wait while his boss partook of a young local. Perhaps there would be a shipment ready and he could choose from one of those. His newest sideline had proven to be one of his most profitable ventures yet.

Rose had been the only woman he'd ever intended to keep for himself. He'd fucked most of the merchandise before sending them on to their new Masters, but he'd always planned to keep her only for himself. Thinking back to the first time he'd seen her walking barefoot along the beach carrying her sandals, he remembered being so enthralled he'd made his driver slow so he could watch her. The sunlight had been peeking through the clouds and seemed to be spotlighting her as she'd strolled down the beach. The gentle Pacific winds had been playing with her long hair and lifting the hem of her skirt to tempt everyone she met with glimpses of her toned thighs. She must have sensed him watching her because she'd turned toward the road. Rose had used her hand to shield her eyes from the sun and scanned the road as if searching out the gaze she'd felt caressing her tanned skin. Raphael watched as she shrugged and resumed her carefree ambling along the water's edge.

It had taken him several months to find out who she was because it seemed the locals liked the young girl and weren't inclined to tell a member of the *Mafioso* about one of their own. Oddly enough, rather than being angry about the small community's protectiveness, he'd found it a bit heartwarming even if it had been damned inconvenient. The fact she was the kind of person who had earned that type of loyalty spoke volumes about her character and had just made him want her all the more. When he'd found out she had a younger brother in need of special training because he was deaf and that her mother was a widow, he knew that he'd found his leverage.

Raphael had never doubted Rose had only agreed to stay with him because he'd sworn to provide for both her brother and her mother. He'd always regretted his youthful mistake of not keeping the promises he'd made to her. If he had taken care of them like he had sworn to, her escape would have been nearly impossible. Her innate sense of family honor was strong and her loyalty to her mother and brother were a powerful tool he'd let slip through his fingers. He wouldn't make the same mistake again. But this time he would plan very carefully. He'd watch her and make sure everything was in place before making a move.

He needed to know who he was dealing with because everything about Kent and Kyle West indicated they might have retired from the military, but they hadn't abandoned the mind-set.

Raphael didn't care if it took him months…he'd already waited ten years…the prize would make the wait well worth it. In the meantime, perhaps he'd find one of the American students studying in the area and ease some of the discomfort between his legs. They were usually more than happy to join him—at least in the beginning. He smiled to himself as he thought of all the ways he could make a woman beg for mercy he'd never grant. He quickly typed in a message to his staff outlining exactly what sort of woman he required up his arrival. There was no question they would provide him with several so he didn't even bother to pick his phone back up when it vibrated against the desk.

Returning his focus to the picture in his hand, he ran his thumb slowly over the image and smiled. "Soon, Rose. Very, very soon."

Chapter Eight

Gracie stood quietly in the beautiful master bathroom as Jax adjusted the temperature of the water in the shower. She'd felt a definite shift in his attitude as he had carried her toward his and Micah's home. The gentle giant that cradled an emotionally exhausted woman to a safe place to rest had faded away. In his place was a man no one would every doubt was a sexual Dominant. His lust-filled eyes traveling down and then back up her body in a slow perusal that she would have sworn sent electric shocks racing up her spine. The look was so intense it felt as if he'd actually touched her. Her sex began to moisten in anticipation and she felt her nipples drawing into tight peaks. *God, he is gorgeous. He is so perfect it feels like he's a figment of my imagination...and if I reach out to touch him, he'll disappear in a puff of smoke.*

His black hair glistened as its gentle waves curled softly at his collar and his eyes seemed to be ever changing in their color. When he was smiling and relaxed she had noticed they were an almost electric blue. But now, they were filled with desire and had shifted to a shade so dark they appeared almost violet. The steam filling the room brought his scent to her in a wave and she felt her sex clench and then flood in response. She had been thrilled to discover he always smelled like a stroll along a sage lined path and the outdoor earthy scent caused her to close her eyes briefly and just breathe him in. Even though he was clearly a Dom, she could sense the sensitive soul below the surface and oddly enough both sides called to her in a way she didn't fully understand.

When he tilted his head slightly to the side and raised an eyebrow, she snapped back to the moment. "Where were you, *Cariña*? You didn't hear anything I said. And if you keep looking at me like that I won't be able to wait until Micah gets here to fuck you." She suspected he'd used the crude words deliberately to shock her, but their impact had been greatly diminished by the fact that it was exactly what she was hoping for.

Gracie was attracted to both Jax and Micah, she had been from the moment they'd met. She'd tried to keep them at arm's length, because it was so much harder to keep secrets from lovers than from friends or casual acquaintances. She'd always known the possibility that she'd have to vanish into the night was lurking just around the corner so keeping ties to a minimum had seemed the easiest. Looking up at Jax, she sighed inwardly and wondered how they'd managed to work themselves past her defenses and into her heart despite her efforts, and quite frankly, she was tired of battling against her desire for them.

Taking a deep breath, Gracie tried to let her fears of Raphael slide to the back of her mind so she could enjoy this time with them. She wanted to make a beautiful memory she could take with her. She needed to focus and remember that at least for this moment she was safe. Gracie wanted to experience the freedom Tobi had talked incessantly about…she wanted to be able to just *let go*. For once, she wanted to let someone else take the reins. And even if it was only for one night, she needed to be able to erase the fear that had weighed her down like an anchor since she'd met Raphael. For one night, she wanted to be able to just feel.

Taking a deep breath, Gracie squared her shoulders and met his gaze. "That's not a threat you know?" She barely recognized her own voice, the huskiness of desire was easy to hear. His eyes widened in surprised for just the briefest of seconds before they went even darker as they clouded over with a primal lust so evident even a woman as inexperienced as Gracie could recognize it.

"Take off your clothes, *Cariña*. Slowly. I want to see you unwrap that lovely body like the gift that it is." He had already removed his shirt, shoes, and socks and he was standing a few feet from her with his dark jeans riding low on narrow hips, giving her a tantalizing peek at the happy trail disappearing under the opened snap of his Levis. His feet were shoulder width apart and his ripped arms crossed over the most amazing chest she'd ever seen. The abs in the shadow of his arms were so defined she wanted to run her tongue along each line. Her mouth had literally watered as she'd watched him pull his shirt over this head. *I want to lick him. I want to know if his skin tastes as delicious as it looks.*

"She's beautiful, isn't she?" Micah's voice startled her out of her thoughts. He was leaning with his shoulder pressed against the doorframe in a pose she knew was intended to look casual, but was anything but. His eyes were filled with intent and locked firmly on hers. She felt the heat of his predatory gaze in every cell. If just having their eyes on her evoked reactions this strong, what on earth would it be like when they touched her? *What am I thinking? I'm totally out of my league with these men.*

"That she is, but she is easily distracted. Seems that it

might be something we'll need to work on." Her eyes darted back to Jax and the glimmer of a smile playing over his full lips relaxed her. She was starting to recognize his teasing tone, but she didn't want to disappoint him either. "I can't say that I ever remember having this much trouble getting a sub in my care out of her clothing though. I may have to rethink my approach to this if I don't start seeing some action pretty quickly."

Gracie might not be experienced in all the protocols of their lifestyle, but she easily recognized a second chance when she saw one. She leaned over and slipped the sandals she'd been wearing from her feet and set them aside. Then slowly lifted her shaking hands to the knot at the back of her neck; struggling with the ties of her halter dress, she was growing frustrated when Jax stepped forward. "Turn around, *Cariña*, let me help you." She turned and shuddered when he moved her hair over her shoulder. He'd started calling her *Cariña* the first night they'd met. His use of a Spanish pet name that meant "beloved" had always touched her heart and she'd always considered it the cornerstone of their bond.

His fingers easily mastered the knot and her dress slid down over her taut nipples like a whispering wave of softness arousing her even further. She could feel how soaked her panties were and she knew it was just a matter of time until they'd be able to see for themselves how aroused she was. As if he'd read her mind, Jax leaned over her shoulder and kissed the tender place behind her ear and whispered, "I can smell your arousal, *Cariña*, and I can't wait to taste you. Now take off those pretty panties unless you want them shredded, because I'm growing very impatient to see you naked."

Gracie's knees went weak at his tone as much as the

words. What was it about these two men that caused her to react to them but not others? She worked alongside several of the Doms from the club and other Alpha males as well, but none of them caused the same throbbing in her sex that these men could create with just a glance.

Tobi had been encouraging her to take a leap of faith and *try*, but it had been a recent offhanded remark that had flipped the script in Gracie's mind. When she'd told Tobi she was worried about what people would think about her if she failed, her sweet friend had informed her, "It isn't any of your business what they think of you, Gracie." The truth of Tobi's statement had stunned her and for several seconds Gracie had literally forgotten to breathe. She had decided right then that she'd wasted enough time trying to live her life in a way that others would find acceptable. There had been something in Tobi's words that had snapped the self-imposed chains Gracie had felt like she'd been dragging everywhere for the past ten years. She was going to have to pick them up again soon enough...but for now, she wanted to feel weightless.

"See what I mean? She just seems to float away. Damnedest thing I've ever seen. Let's see if I can't get her attention back on us, shall we?" Jax's voice registered on some level of her subconscious, but it was the sound of fabric ripping that brought her back to the moment. Glancing down, she saw her panties laying in tatters on the floor. *Holy shit!*

Gracie had been poor for so long she was devastated at what he'd done. Blinking rapidly, she tried to hold back the tears but they breached her lower lids and slid down her cheeks. Both men were immediately standing in front of her. The guilt on Jax's face a stark contrast to the desire she'd seen in his eyes just seconds ago.

"*Cariña*, did I hurt you?" She felt bad for worrying him, but damn, money had never come easy for her and those were the first panties she'd ever had that hadn't come from Walmart. *Freddie-Fuckedy Fuck!*

"No, you didn't hurt me. But those cost me eight dollars. They were the first ones I bought at a store that didn't also sell groceries and sporting goods. Shit, they were the first ones I've ever had that didn't have a picture of fruit on the damned label." For the first time since she'd met him, Micah leaned his head back and roared with laughter. Gracie felt her face heat as embarrassment flooded her. Leaning down, she picked up her dress and started putting it back on. *Damn. What made me think I could do this? These guys are trained Doms. They deal with rich, beautiful women all the time. Why would they want a short, chunky woman who wears clothing purchased from bargain bins?* All Gracie could think about was how naïve she'd been and even though she didn't ordinarily drink, she was certain she'd earned the right after today. As soon as she got back to her little cabin she planned to drink the last of the tequila Tobi left after their last margarita party. She only hoped there was enough of the amber liquid to numb the humiliation.

JAX WATCHED AS embarrassment washed over Gracie's face and he hoped like hell Micah pulled his head out of his ass soon and realized what he'd done. They usually didn't interfere with each other during a scene, but this was shaping up to be an epic cluster fuck if he didn't make an exception. When she stood back up after retrieving her dress from the floor, Jax wrapped his hand around her wrist and stilled her. "*Cariña*, I really do believe you are misinterpreting Micah's laughter." He heard Micah go dead silent beside him. *That's right, dumbass, pay attention.* "And one of the most important parts of any relationship is communication, and as we've said it is particularly true in ménages, so I think you should ask him to clarify his reaction before you make your decision."

Standing in front of her and seeing the humiliation in her eyes, Jax wanted to whack his partner right upside the head. Micah was a lot of things and the truth was sometimes he *could be* a real arrogant asshat. But in all the years Jax had known him, he'd never known his friend to deliberately hurt a sub's feelings, so he didn't think that had been Micah's intent this time either. But damn it, Micah really needed to get his head back in this thing before she stormed out of their cabin and they lost their chance with her. When Jax looked over at Micah, he was shocked at his confused expression. *Really? You don't know what you did? What a goat-fuck.*

"Grace? What is this about? Why are you angry?" Jax just shook his head at his friend. *Yep, he's an idiot.*

Gracie turned to him and Jax smiled when she closed her eyes briefly. It was clear she was trying to call upon every ounce of her patience. When she opened them again fire danced in the beautiful gray orbs. "Are you fucking kidding me? Really? You think I am that dim? Did you set me up for this? Was there some sort of plan to," he saw her eyes go even wider as if she'd just had some kind of *aha moment,* "oh no...oh, I'll strangle her...I swear I will. Friend or not, if Tobi set you up to spend time with me I'll bat her a good one before I disappear."

Now Jax felt every bit as confused as Micah looked. But it was time to shut her little hissy down. *"Stop!"* His one word command had been loud, clear, and filled with enough bite to get her attention. "*Cariña*, drop the dress and listen closely." Jax was pleased to see her fingers open and the dress flutter to the floor again so quickly he wasn't sure her mind had even had time to register the command before her body had obeyed. "Tobi has nothing to do with you standing gloriously naked in this bathroom. Now, explain to Master Micah exactly why you are angry and do it respectfully or you're going to earn yourself a spanking before we even begin." Jax watched her eyes widen and her pupils dilate. *Perfect*.

Chapter Nine

MICAH WAS COMPLETELY dumbfounded and he damned well hated the feeling. After years of acing every imaginable type of military training designed to ready him for any contingency, he loathed feeling like he was unprepared for whatever was happening around him. He stared at Gracie and waited. She was obviously battling her anger and frustration back enough to speak. The comments she'd made about her underwear had caught him so off guard and that brief glimpse at her sense of humor had warmed him to the point he'd burst out laughing from the sheer pleasure of it all.

However, now—when she looked up at him, her eyes flooded with tears and they harbored so much resentment, he was shocked. Her voice trembled, but she spoke clearly. "I…well, I know that I'm not as uptown as the women you usually deal with. I'm not rich and the few nice things I have mean something to me. And just because you don't think they are valuable…well, it just isn't nice to make fun of people who have less than you." She'd started out looking directly at him, but as she'd continued speaking her voice had gotten softer and her eyes had dropped until she was looking at the floor. Micah could count on one hand the number of times he'd been this completely blindsided and stunned into complete horror knowing he'd hurt another person. His heart broke for her and knowing he was the cause of the pain he'd seen in her expression almost made him physically ill.

Stepping forward, he lifted her chin with his fingers. "I want you to listen very carefully to what I'm telling you, baby. I laughed at the funny way you described your underwear and I thoroughly enjoyed getting a glimpse at your wicked sense of humor. Most of the subs at the club are so vain they'd never dream of calling it anything but lingerie and I doubt most of them have any clue what can be purchased at Walmart." He gave her a few seconds to process what he'd said before continuing, "Now, before I address your *uptown* remark, I want to know exactly what it means so we don't set ourselves up for another misunderstanding."

He listened as she listed a litany of traits and he bristled on the inside at the accuracy of many of her observations. He and Jax did usually play with trained submissives who were generally college educated, professional women from moneyed families. They hadn't intentionally chosen tall, slender women but looking back he realized most of the women they'd been with fit that body type. He suddenly felt very shallow, and knowing she'd read them so clearly made his epiphany even more humbling.

"You are right, we usually do play with wealthy, professional women, but not for the reason you're thinking. The membership fees for The Prairie Winds Club are quite substantial and that alone limits the women we come into contact with. And I think we've unconsciously chosen taller women because I'm tall and Jax is a fucking giant." She grinned and he was relieved to see her beginning to relax. "But if you'd stop and think about that, you'd realize how much more special that makes you."

Micah let his words linger for a moment as he took a

step closer and ran the back of his fingers around the outside curve of her breast. He saw her pulse pounding at the base of her throat and the steam from the shower was settling on her skin making it look like it had been kissed by the morning dew. "Your body is rocking, there is no doubt about that, but it's the woman inside that fascinates us both. And I haven't enjoyed a good laugh like that in a long time and I thank you for it. I'm sorry you thought it was at your expense." Micah had always believed that apologies were best when they were simple and straightforward and that was exactly how he'd tried to keep this one. "Now, let's get you into that shower before there isn't any hot water left."

They were forced to rush through their showers, but they'd both promised her water sports next time. Their shower was large, but it was nothing like the one in Kent and Kyle's apartment atop the club. And since the elder Wests had recently agreed to give Micah and Jax a permanent lease on a couple of acres and the large building at the front of the ranch they'd recently purchased, they'd be enjoying a larger shower soon enough. The property was directly adjacent to Prairie Winds and the architect had recently finished the plans for adding on and remodeling the large open building. He smiled to himself thinking about the playroom they'd included in the plans. There would also be plenty of space for their rapidly expanding security business and a luxury living quarters as well.

As they patted Gracie's damp skin with soft towels, the sweet scent of her arousal filled the air and Micah felt his cock harden in response. He could tell she was nervous. He kissed the back of her hand as they led her out of the bathroom and saw her surprised look when they bypassed the bed. Instead, settling her on the small sofa facing the natural stone fireplace. While it didn't often get bitterly cold in their area, when the temps neared freezing everyone felt it to their bones because they weren't accustomed to lower temperatures. Micah grabbed the remote and started the gas fire and let the warmth wash over them. Jax pulled her onto his lap and adjusted the plush robe they'd given her so her breasts were partially exposed to their view.

Micah watched her shift on Jax's lap and held back his laughter at the pained expression he saw move over this friend's face. "Do you know what a safe word is, baby?" To her credit, she nodded quickly and proceeded to recite a near perfect textbook definition of the term, including when it should be used. He nodded and fought to hold back his grin at her enthusiasm. "You are exactly right. We'll use the club's stop light system that you just defined perfectly." Micah smiled when her cheeks flushed. "Jax and I enjoy a wide variety of play, and we'll cover everything in detail later. But for now, you need to know we will not leave permanent marks or draw blood." He saw her shudder and Jax tightened his hold on her briefly before letting her sit back up straight. Micah's next question made her eyes widen briefly before her cheeks turned a lovely shade of pink. "Are you on birth control?" He'd already seen her medical file because a physical was a condition of her employment at the Forum Shops, but he wanted to be sure that hadn't changed in the past few weeks.

To her credit, she didn't hesitate to answer, "Yes. And well, as you probably know, my doctor's report was clean." She suddenly looked at the floor as if embarrassed and Micah used his finger to bring her chin back up so she was forced to meet his eyes. When he simply raised his brow in question, she continued, "And...I haven't been with anyone since my physical, but you already know that as well." And they had been fairly certain that was the case because she'd only been away from Prairie Winds twice, both times with Tobi, and they knew no visitors had come through the front gates to see her. He and Jax had discussed the fact that she seemed to lead a very lonely existence, and that made a lot more sense now that they knew she'd been in hiding.

Refocusing on the discussion, Micah caressed the side of her face as he spoke, "We are both clean as well, and we would rather not use condoms unless you have a particular fondness for them." Personally, he hated the artificial feel of latex, but had never played without them, and their use inside the club was a hard and fast rule. But Gracie wasn't a woman they were planning to scene with and then walk away from either and the difference that created in their viewpoint was staggering.

When she'd agreed to forgo the condoms, he nodded and Jax brushed a soft kiss over her temple. Micah and Jax had discussed various ways to approach things tonight and numerous alternatives as well. While Jax was more willing to fly by the seat of his pants, Micah was much more comfortable having a plan—and a couple of spares was all the better. They had deliberately not spoken with Tobi about Gracie, preferring at least for the time being to explore the attraction between them as they would with any other woman who had caught their interest. That wasn't to say they wouldn't seek her input if things hit a rough patch, but for now they planned to rely on their instincts.

Jax was rubbing slow circles over her lower back and Micah could see her eyelids fluttering with fatigue. It was time to make love to her and then let her get some rest.

Micah was looking forward to holding her almost as much as he was burying himself inside her sweet heat, and that realization startled him. Giving Jax a quick nod to let him know it was time to proceed, Micah reached forward and slid his hand inside her robe to cup her breasts with his hands. She wasn't a large woman, but her breasts were very round, full, and high. Her skin was amazingly smooth and the weight of her breasts as they fit against his palms felt perfect. He never took his eyes off hers as he continued to caress her and when he brushed his thumbs over her budded nipples, she gasped. Her eyes darkened from their usual gray to a shade that looked like the turbulent clouds of an approaching storm in the west Texas sky. *So responsive.*

Micah had been watching as her long hair dried, and the soft waves of black silk caught the dimmed lights. The natural shine of her tresses reflected the amber light back into the room and the ever-changing patterns were fascinating. He'd always thought Jax had the blackest hair he'd ever seen, but hers was an even deeper shade. His own hair had always been a sandy blonde that bleached out quickly and always made him look like a displaced surfer. The color had certainly made it difficult for him to disappear in a crowd in most of the hot spots he'd been assigned as a SEAL.

"Tonight is about you, baby. We will be focused on your needs, but we'll also be indulging our own, because you are just simply too wonderful to resist. There will be times in the future when we'll cater to our own needs above yours for a variety of reasons, but usually it's as simple as…because we can. But tonight we want to show you how precious your submission is." He smiled at her and knew that she'd read enough about Dominance and submission to understand exactly what he was telling her. And he was happier than he wanted to admit that she hadn't corrected him when he'd referred to her submission to them. His heart had recognized her as theirs that first night when she'd reacted so perfectly to him grasping her wrist. Just that brief bit of restraint had triggered an immediate response that even a Dom new to the lifestyle would have easily recognized. And her instant connection to Jax had sealed her fate.

Chapter Ten

JAX HAD MOVED with a fluid grace that defied his size and Gracie felt the cool sheets caress her back when he laid her on the bed. She'd noticed the size of the bed when they'd walked past it earlier, but now that she was in it with both Micah and Jax along each side, it didn't seem as overwhelming. "Your bed is huge, but I can see why, you are both large men."

Jax had grinned at her and she noticed his eyes had darkened. His voice was softer and the huskiness made her sex clench. "Oh, *Cariña*, we each have our own bedrooms. This room is for you. We'll only use it when you are here with us." He leaned forward and she watched his pink tongue as he licked around her areola and then blew a soft puff of air over it. She gasped at the sensation and he smiled when the skin puckered tightly. "Your nipples are so perfect. Their dusty rose color fascinates me and their intense responses to our touch makes me anxious to see them in beautiful jewel-weighted clamps." Gracie arched her back in an unconscious bid for his attention and he seemed more than happy to comply. In her peripheral view, she noticed Micah was moving down the bed and her entire body felt like it was shimmering with need. She wondered briefly where he was headed and then she felt him settle between her legs. *Oh Lord of all things holy, surely he isn't planning to start there.*

"Open for me, baby. Let me see your pretty, pink pussy." Gracie's body must have registered Micah's words, because she'd opened her legs before her mind had even processed what he'd said. His voice had been barely above a whisper, but there was no question it was a command.

JAX COULD SEE the questions in Gracie's eyes, but what she didn't know was how much Micah loved the taste of a woman's pussy. Micah had never made a secret of how addictive he considered the tangy syrup of a woman's arousal. And once he'd made a sub come, Jax knew he would lap up his creamy prize with abandon. Jax wasn't the aficionado that Micah was, but he couldn't wait to taste Gracie. Just the ambrosia of her arousal was enough to send his need spiraling toward heaven. In his peripheral vision, Jax saw Micah settle himself between Gracie's legs, widen and bend her knees so her feet were flat on the bed. When she started to lift her head Jax stilled her with a kiss and when he pulled back he smiled at her half-lidded lust-filled eyes. He loved seeing her lost in a fog of desire and vowed to himself that they would keep her under the two of them as much as possible.

Brushing his lips against the side of face, he inhaled against her hair. God, he loved the feeling of soft skin against his and their soap smelled a lot better on her that it did on either of them. "Tell me what Master Micah is doing to you, *Cariña*." Jax watched her eyes go wide and then her breath seemed to come rushing from her lungs in a series of strangled cries. He knew exactly what Micah was doing and he doubted very much Gracie was going to be able to speak coherently much longer.

"Oh my God, he is licking me and sucking on…it's…oh it is just so perfect. I had no idea it would feel…oh Jesus Lord of all things holy…it feels sooo good…like electricity racing through me, but better." Jax knew his smile was breaking through but he simply couldn't hold it back. She was so damned responsive, and her words so honest and genuine that he was just over the top pleased.

Just as she opened her mouth to speak again, Jax rolled and then pinched both nipples between his fingers and commanded, "Come for us, *Cariña*." Her back bowed off the bed so far that Jax heard Micah's growl of frustration as he placed his hand on her lower abdomen and pressed her back in position. Her skin flushed the most beautiful shade of deep pink that he'd ever seen. Thank God they lived on a property housing a sex club where anyone hearing her scream would recognize it for what it was and know exactly what was happening.

Jax could hear Micah humming in satisfaction against the petals of her labia and couldn't wait for his turn to taste her. Swirling his tongue around her distended nipples, he said, "That was the hottest thing I've ever seen. Watching you shatter in release was perfect, love. You didn't hold back your responses and that pleases us both very much." Both he and Micah were well-endowed men and they wanted her relaxed and sated before they slid into her tight sheath. Jax outlined her lips with the tip of his tongue before slamming his mouth over hers and plunging his tongue into her mouth. It was a no holds barred kiss and even though he'd intended to keep things soft and light, his body was consumed with a primal need for her and had simply taken over.

For the first time in all the years he'd been a Dom, his body's craving had been greater than his mind's ability to control it and he lost himself in his exploration of each dip and crevice of her sweet mouth. The softness of her lips and the sweetness of her sighs as he took her by storm were tantamount to throwing gas on a fire. He felt like he'd been plunged into an inferno and the heat was consuming every bit of his restraint. By the time his need for oxygen registered, Jax was breathless. Pulling back from her was sweet torture but he was almost buzzing with anticipation just thinking about finally getting to watch Micah fuck her. "I'm going to enjoy watching your other Master fuck you, *Cariña*, and then I'm going to finish up this evenings activities by taking you right back up that mountain. And when we reach the top we'll take that leap together, love."

Micah moved over her and watched as Gracie looked up at him. Her expression was a combination of surprise and satisfaction that made him smile. Knowing he'd put that look in her eyes, seeing her eyes so wide—her expression dazed made him want to beat his chest in triumph. He was fairly sure she wasn't entirely able to focus yet and when she felt the tip of his cock barely brush over her opening, her entire body seemed to come back to the moment. Gracie's moaned, "Please," told him the instant she became fully aware of his position. Seeing her honest, open response, and the look of wonder as she tried to center her mind on the sensations bombarding her, was intoxicating to watch. He knew she hadn't even known what she was asking for, but her sweet, luscious body knew exactly what it needed, and it didn't seem to mind forging ahead even if her mind wasn't fully on board yet.

For the first time in years, Micah felt an emotional connection to the woman beneath him. He'd spent years enjoying the pleasures of sex, but the satisfaction had only been physical. And lately, even that had left him feeling hollow inside. Looking into Gracie's face, he hoped she would see the difference he was feeling. Every single thing that had happened from the very first moment he'd met Gracie had led them to this moment, to the emotion that even the most dedicated skeptic could have seen being slowly building between the three of them. The bond that had started forming while they'd been getting to know each other as friends was already stronger than any he'd ever experienced before, and he knew they'd barely scratched the surface.

Micah had always been content to stay hidden comfortably behind his Dom persona. Letting "Master Micah" be the only side the subs he'd played with ever get to see. There hadn't been any reason to become emotionally entangled because he'd never wanted to spend more than an hour or two meeting their mutual desires. But everything with Gracie was different. The truth of Dean West's words continued to float through his mind. The elder West had been dead on—finding *the one* and feeling it to the depths of his soul was a rush like nothing else he'd ever experienced. God knew Micah was every bit as big an adrenaline junky as every other Special Forces soldier out there. But this? Oh this was definitely a bigger kick than anything he'd ever experienced.

Placing his hands on either side of her face, Micah focused all of his intention on her and settled just enough of his weight against her that she'd feel his rigid length pressing against her. He wanted her to feel safe in the shelter of his embrace, but to also know he was in control.

And the best way he knew to be sure her full attention remained zeroed in on his face was to keep his eyes totally focused on hers. He was close enough that she'd feel his breath brush against her lips when he spoke. "I want you. I want you with an intensity that is unlike anything I've ever experienced. The depth of my need for you is so unique that I'm humbled by it." He held himself still and took a couple of steadying breaths hoping to rein in his almost overwhelming desire to sink into her and fuck her into the mattress. The urge to plunder her was nearly irresistible. "I'm trying to love you slowly, but I'm walking a fine edge here, baby, and I need you to cooperate because I don't want to hurt you." Her eyes had gone from lust-filled to desperate. He'd seen more than one sub hurt because bodies took over and their need to "get on with it" smothered any hint of self-preservation. On several occasions, he'd seen subs tear delicate tissues and the results were never pleasant.

Rocking his hips forward just enough to penetrate her slightly, Micah was grateful for the release she'd just experienced because it was providing the lubrication he needed to glide smoothly between her swollen tissues. Keeping his eyes on hers, he watched her intently—waiting for that one moment when he knew she'd crossed the line and he'd need to be prepared for her sudden movement. Deciding that distraction was his best alternative, he asked, "How long has it been for you, baby?"

She closed her eyes and just for a second he wasn't sure if she was ashamed of her answer or if she was just trying to bring the question into focus so she could answer. "Five years." He went completely still, he was barely breathing. Blinking several times, he tried to decide if he'd actually heard her correctly. *Five years? Is she fucking serious? Were the men in Austin blind?* Micah knew she was twenty-six and that was a long time considering her age and the glimpses he'd seen of the passionate woman lurking just below the surface. "My twenty-first birthday to be exact." She took a deep breath and he could see her mentally sliding right out of the mood he and Jax had worked so hard to set.

"Well, let's see what we can do about replacing that memory with something better, shall we? My cock is pressing against a warm, wet, welcoming entrance and I can feel the heat surrounding me and I'm not even inside yet." As he began rocking his hips back and forth, he slid into her in small increments, gaining depth with each stroke. He felt the sweat beading on his brow and the effort it was taking to hold back from plunging deep was testing him in ways he hadn't explored in a very long time.

Micah listened to each little moan and sigh Gracie made and relished the satisfaction it gave him knowing he was giving her pleasure. Her body had returned to the pliable state it had been in before she'd mentioned her twenty-first birthday, and he was enjoying every inch of her softening channel as he pressed steadily inside. Feeling her tight muscles stretch to accommodate his cock was sweet indeed.

"Relax, baby...let me in. Those rippling muscles are already driving my control right over the edge. You're so hot and wet...and when you squeeze me as I'm pulling out it feels like you are caressing me with wet, silk covered desire. It rocks me to my very soul." Micah was sure he'd never spoken any words that he'd meant more than those he'd just uttered, and he just let his heart fill itself with her.

Everything with Gracie was different...he hadn't had sex without a condom since he was a teenager and the feeling of connection from the skin to skin contact was unlike anything he'd ever experienced. *I'll never be able to fuck another woman again. This one holds everything that I am in the palm of her hands.*

When Micah slid his arms under Gracie's knees and lifted, her pelvis tilted just enough to change the angle of his thrusts and send the corona of his penis over her G-spot on each stroke. The rigid ring around the head was the perfect stimulus and he could sense her arousal ratchet up exponentially. Watching Gracie lose all focus as she surrendered the last of her inhibitions was the most erotic thing Micah had ever seen. Her torso was flushed a gorgeous deep rose, her eyes half-lidded and unfocused, and she seemed to almost glow from the inside out.

He'd never really held any fondness for straight vanilla sex before…it had just never flipped any switches for him. But this was off the chart perfect and just as her internal muscles clamped down on him like a vice, he shouted her name and let the fire that had been boiling in his testicles rocket out of his cock drenching Gracie's clenched channel in blasts meant to claim her as his own. Hearing her scream his name had only added to his satisfaction and for long seconds he wasn't even sure he'd be able to draw in a breath.

When his brain finally kicked in and ordered his lungs to pull in the oxygen it was craving, Micah lifted off her and smiled. Several gasping breaths later, he finally managed to rasp out, "There are simply no words to describe that, baby. Anything I'd say wouldn't do justice to how incredible you are." Seeing her eyes fill with tears, he knew she'd felt the same melding. He leaned back down and pressed his lips to her tear streaked cheeks and savored the salty flavor. "Jax and I will always be nearby to kiss away your tears, sweetheart. Whether they are tears of joy or sadness—we'll be right beside you."

Turning her toward Jax, Micah moved back and watched in wonder as the most amazing woman he'd ever met melted against his best friend. *She's perfect and she is ours. If anyone hurts her, I'll move heaven and hell to take them apart.*

Chapter Eleven

Jax had visited sex clubs all over the world and hadn't thought he'd ever see anything that would top some of the eroticism he'd witnessed. He'd always been in awe of other nations whose sexual freedoms and openness far exceeded those in the United States. Even many of the stricter religious states where they'd fought were remarkably open minded about what was acceptable behind closed doors. But watching his best friend make love to Gracie had blown away everything he'd ever believed was "hot" and he knew those images would be etched in his memory for the rest of his life. Seeing Micah and Gracie's expressions as their souls linked together was as close to magic as Jax had ever witnessed.

Micah was one of the most astute sexual Dominants Jax had ever known. His ability to "read" a sub was almost legendary. He could catch even the most subtle shifts in body language and interpret the meaning with unerring accuracy, but Jax had never known Micah to connect on an emotional level with any woman. So seeing him make that connection with Gracie had been amazing. Jax waited as Micah spoke softly to Gracie while she waded through the emotional aftermath of what had obviously been an earth-shattering release.

When Micah turned her slowly into Jax's arms, it felt like he'd finally "come home". The rightness of the moment was only eclipsed by the surge of blood into his already engorged cock that left him almost light-headed. Feeling her naked perfection pressed against him, her pillowy breasts against his chest with his cock trapped between them caused him to groan in pleasure. Sighing at the loss of her warmth, he pulled back so he could look into her eyes. "*Cariña*, do you need something to drink? A snack? A break? It won't be the end of the world if you are too tired to continue tonight." Stroking his fingers lightly down the side of her face, he watched as she seemed to consider his words.

"I'd like to get a drink and maybe a small snack. I suppose you noticed I didn't eat much dinner. But then I would like to continue because I might not get another chance and...well, I don't want to always regret the missed opportunity." Jax had to bite the inside of his mouth to keep from telling her there was no way in fucking hell she was leaving them. It was too early in their relationship for either he or Micah to issue orders or make those demands. They would just have to convince her that staying at Prairie Winds was the best and safest option.

Jax knew too well that his size alone was often intimidating and if he was reading her right, she'd already been a bit skittish about him fitting inside her. It was easy to see how vulnerable and emotionally raw she was feeling, so letting her get her bearings was in everyone's best interest. He just nodded his head in understanding as he helped her to her feet. Looking over her head, he saw Micah's scowl and Jax could only hope his friend would give her a minute to settle before saying anything to send up her defenses. Considering what they'd learned about her past, it was obvious she'd been forced to learn quickly how to shut herself off from people as a matter of safety, and all those years of conditioning weren't going to be undone overnight.

Jax had purposely not mentioned her comment about leaving while they'd eaten a light snack and enjoyed a bit of wine. Once the wine had worked its magic, Jax could see the tension draining from Gracie's body language. Leaning back in his chair watching her as she picked up the last piece of cheese, he thought back on how mortified he and the others had been by the lack of food in her small apartment. She'd left a pay stub out laying on her dresser and he'd been stunned when he'd seen how little she'd been living on. Hell, it was a fucking miracle she hadn't been homeless. And seeing how little she'd been earning had certainly explained her lack of food. No one had been surprised to see how easily she'd tired when she'd first moved to Prairie Winds. Jax smiled to himself remembering how happy their entire team had been when Gracie had started to blossom in good health after moving to Prairie Winds. Sometimes the "mother hen instincts" of all those Special Forces soldiers amazed and amused him.

It was time to tackle the subject of her leaving and Jax was pleased that Micah seemed willing to let him handle it. "You know what I've noticed, Gracie?" She looked up at him and her blinking stare and deer in the headlights look told him she'd gone on point immediately so he didn't leave her wondering. "It seems like you've gotten healthier since you've been living at Prairie Winds. You seem to have more energy and your color is better. Why do you suppose that is?"

A part of Jax's training in the Special Forces had focused on interrogation techniques and he intended to use those skills shamelessly now. He wanted to help Gracie see what he and Micah already knew—that she was far safer here with them even if Raphael Baldamino knew her location. There were very few places on earth he'd consider safer for her and she damned well wouldn't have access to any of those, so she was going to stay right where she was. Micah had already set things in motion to provide Gracie's mother and brother with protection until they knew what they were up against. The most logical way for Baldamino to bring Gracie to heel would be to use her family's safety as leverage, and no one was going to allow that to happen.

Gracie had been chewing her bottom lip and was obviously trying to figure out his angle. In Jax's view, if she was trying to figure out the "correct way" to answer his question, they hadn't built enough trust yet. He took her hand in his and drew lazy circles in her palm with his thumb. "*Cariña*, stop over-thinking the question." Her gaze returned to him quickly and the lights reflected in her dark eyes.

Gracie was a very bright woman and Jax couldn't help but compare her with Kent and Kyle West's mother and wife. Lilly and Tobi West were both intelligent and spirited. He'd heard their husbands mention on more than one occasion how "getting them out of their own heads" was often the biggest challenge during scenes. At the time, Jax hadn't fully understood what his friends and their dads meant, but it was abundantly clear now.

Gracie's agitated voice broke through his thoughts, "Well fiddle farts. You're not going to let this go, are you?" He didn't even bother to respond, and he noticed Micah had just crossed his arms over his chest, waiting. After a dramatic sigh that nearly caused him to roll his eyes at her theatrics, she finally continued, "I agree that Prairie Winds has been great for me. I'm eating better and sleeping a lot better because it's quiet." *And safe,* even though she hadn't said it out loud, the unspoken admission still sounded loud and clear in Jax's mind. He wasn't going to let her off the hook because he knew there was more to it than that, and it was obvious that she knew it as well. She took another deep breath and seemed to have become terribly interested in the wood frame around the window she was standing next to.

GRACIE WANTED TO reach over and smack Jax upside the head, but she was fairly sure that wouldn't work out well for her. Even though she had only read about Doms and subs in the hundreds of books on Tobi's e-reader, it didn't take a rocket scientist to see where that would lead.

Anytime she or her younger brother, Alex, were being "buttheads" their mom would pop them just enough to "rattle their brains back into gear". *Holy horse feathers I'm turning into my mom.* Gracie wasn't a fool, she knew exactly where Jax was leading her with his questions, and in all honesty, there probably wasn't a whole lot she could do to avoid the inevitable conclusion. But damn-it-all-to-hell she wasn't going to make it easy on him if she could avoid it.

Looking over her shoulder seeking out Micah had proven useless when she saw he had adopted a "stop avoiding the question" expression similar to Jax's. Jax had stepped back from her and now both men were standing with their bare feet shoulder width apart in nothing but faded Levi's. The top buttons were open and the starkly different hues of the delicious trail pointing south was enough to make a girl's mouth water. Neither had bothered to put on a shirt and the sight of their bare, muscular chests was a distraction of Biblical proportions. Jax's pectoral muscles reminded her of large pillows with nipples and she suddenly realized she was staring at his chest grinning like a fool. When her eyes finally returned his, he was smiling at her indulgently.

"Like what you see, *Cariña*?" His voice had lost some of its earlier edge, his tone was now more lusty than demanding. *Oh boy, do I ever! Let's can the chitchat and get back to the fun stuff.*

"Well, yeah. You both know you're hot. And you know perfectly well what effect you have on women. Don't play that lame card with me, Jax." Gracie didn't even realize she'd put her hands on her hips until she saw his eyes flick down to her chest. They'd given her a thin cotton button down shirt to wear but hadn't let her button it. When she'd moved her hands to her hips she'd inadvertently moved the shirt open enough to bare her ample cleavage and bare sex. Watching his nostrils flare and his eyes dilate sent a bolt of electric need straight to her pussy and she felt it flood with cream. *I swear it is as if my body belongs to them instead of me when they are near.* The realization that accompanied that thought was so startling she actually gasped.

In an instant Micah was standing shoulder to shoulder with Jax in front of her and their looks were ones of concern rather than desire. *Way to spoil the mood, Rose. Oh no…no…oh, God.* Realizing that she'd actually thought of herself as Rose was so frightening that she swayed on her feet. The single most important thing she'd learned after escaping Raphael was that even thinking of herself in terms of her former identity was dangerous. Before she could even blink Micah had scooped her up into his arms and moved to the living room sofa, settling her on his lap.

Jax sat close and pulled her hands into his own. "Tell us what went through your mind, *Cariña*, and don't you dare lie." When she looked down and hesitated, he put his finger under her chin and brought her attention back to his face. "And Grace, we *will* know if you lie. You also need to remember, lying by omission or editing your response will be punished just as if you'd told us that grass is purple."

Sighing, she explained exactly how unsettling she found their power over her and how devastating it was that she'd actually thought of herself as Rose Rivera. She was immensely relieved at how understanding they'd been. And even though they'd glossed over her comments about how they affected her, she hadn't missed the gleam of satisfaction in their eyes. And they had both agreed that seeing herself as Rose was a dangerous mind-set to embrace, at least for the time being. Jax had brushed her hair over her shoulder in a tender move that hinted at an even deeper intimacy and she loved how settling she found it was to have them touching her. Jax's voice was low and full of concern, but she knew his confidence in the words was bone deep, "*Cariña*, let us help you. This is what we do."

Micah moved her face to his and spoke softly, "We're already providing your mother and brother with protection because it's reasonable to assume they will be Baldamino's first line of attack to bring you in."

Gracie felt as if ice water had suddenly replaced her blood. God in heaven how had she deluded herself to believe if she just disappeared her family would be safe? And now that she'd heard Micah's assessment out loud, it all seemed crystal clear and the flash of fear that raced up her spine felt as if she'd been electrocuted. *Why didn't I take that seriously? How could I have been so naïve? Raphael would never leave mama and Alex alone. They won't ever be safe because my love for them makes them the perfect leverage.* She hadn't even realized she was beginning to panic until she'd felt Jax's hands tighten around her own and heard his stern, "Grace. Stop. Now."

He let go of her hands and placed his on her cheeks, and leaned forward until they were practically nose-to-nose. "Breathe with me." Her mind was whirling at the thought of being forced to return to Costa Rica with Raphael. All she could see was the room she'd been held in for so long and it was whirling around her like a tornado. She gulped in great gasping breaths feeling as if she'd suddenly been thrust on to a spinning ride that was slowly tipping to the side. Before she fell all the way into the abyss of the stark terror flashing all around her, a sharp pinch to her nipples brought her focus back to Jax's hardened expression. "That's better. Stay with us, Gracie. We need for you to understand the dangers, but not be paralyzed by them. Now breathe with me." After a few minutes of slow, measured breaths Gracie felt as if the ride had slowed down enough she could jump off the damned thing and at least get her feet back under her.

It took several attempts before she could finally manage to push words past her lips. "I-I understand. But I hadn't considered how much danger mama and Alex would be in. Alex won't hear them coming…and mama will die trying to protect him." She blinked back the tears that threatened to spill over as she tried to gather her thoughts. Everything about this was just so screwed up that she didn't even know where to begin. And it all began because she'd been walking along the beach one afternoon enjoying the cool breeze gliding over the crystalline water of the Pacific as it moved in gentle, lapping waves onto the shore.

It had been so hot that whole summer and that day's more moderate temperature had seemed like a heaven-sent invitation. She loved walking along the beach. There was something about the rhythm of the never-ending surf that seemed to settle everything within her, almost as if it were resetting her soul…bringing everything back into synch.

Micah stood abruptly, and with her cradled safely in his arms, he made his way back down the hall. Over his shoulder he spoke to Jax, amusement obvious in his tone. "I don't know what we're going to do about our woman. One minute, she is racing toward a panic attack like she's driving a Formula 500 racecar and the next, she is gazing off into space as if she were remembering her favorite childhood hideaway. I have a couple of suggestions to remind her of the importance of staying in the moment when she is with us, but I'm not sure she's ready for the paddling she deserves." She felt his chest vibrate against her as he chuckled at her gasped indignation. "I don't know, Jax, maybe you just need to fuck her senseless. And then when she is too tired to wiggle, and her mind won't work on more than one track at a time, we'll be able to reason with her. It's suddenly becoming crystal clear what all four of the Wests mean when they say their women tended to float off in their own thoughts."

If Gracie hadn't spent these last few weeks getting to know Micah and Jax, she might have been worried by his words, but she could easily hear the teasing in his voice. And if she was honest, she'd admit that his words sent tingles to all her girly parts in very short order.

Chapter Twelve

SITTING IN KENT and Kyle West's office the next morning waiting for everyone to assemble, Gracie lost herself in sweet memories of the night before. Jax had been so thoughtful, yet hadn't let her hide, even from herself. And Micah had more than made up for laughing at her comments. And then after the break they'd taken, the two of them had actually made her come twice before Jax had even attempted penetrating her. She'd been grateful because even though they were both large men, the fact was Jax was huge, and not just in height. Her body had stretched to accommodate him, but she had known his patience had certainly been tested. Gracie could still close her eyes and see the strain in his expression as he leaned over her. His slow penetration had let her tissues welcome him with warmth, and she'd been nearly wild with need by the time he was pressed against her cervix.

It hadn't mattered how much she'd begged, he'd stayed in control. Pulling from her body with excruciating precision and then sliding back in with tortuously slow strokes, Jax had sent her over the edge of release again before he'd finally fucked her with enough force to catapult her back into the abyss of a screaming orgasm that had stolen her ability to move. She was so lost in the naughty memory that she hadn't even noticed Tobi sitting next to her until her friend laughed. "Holy harp playing Hannah, if that isn't the look of a well fucked woman, I don't know what is."

Kyle's stern voice sounded from the doorway behind them, "Tobi, that's one."

Tobi cringed and said, "Dam…s and reservoirs, I swear he has dog ears." Gracie was fairly sure she'd heard Kyle growl but she resisted the urge to turn and look at him. "I know we can't talk here, but I want you to know you aren't off the hook. I want details later, and you better not leave anything out." Tobi West was a bundle of pure energy wrapped in a petite blonde package and Gracie thanked God each day for her friendship. Watching Tobi struggle with everything life had thrown at her had kept things in perspective for Gracie, and having her close as the men started discussing security measures was reassuring. The entire security team had let the two of them sit together and talk quietly while they'd explained the situation to two deputies and Parker Andrews. Gracie recognized Parker as one of the club members, but she hadn't known he was a police captain until Tobi had whispered it to her.

"Isn't he a cutie? We have to find him a sub." Gracie could already see Tobi's matchmaking set itself in motion and a part of her almost felt sorry for the man. She'd never seen either of the deputies before and they seemed nervous about being there so Gracie was sure they weren't members of Prairie Winds Club. Tobi must have noticed her unease with the other two officers because she leaned close and whispered, "They are friends of Kent and Kyle's. I think they are interested in becoming members also. Don't worry, honey, you know my husbands wouldn't have them here if they didn't trust them. Besides, it was some sort of jurisdiction issue so Parker can only advise. I don't care about those details, I just want you to be safe. Don't you even think about leaving here, I swear I'll hunt your ass down myself."

"Tobi, that's two." This time it was Kent's admonishment that had Tobi cringing.

"Well froggy farts, I hate it when they tag-team." Gracie could only shake her head at Tobi's antics. She also knew full well that her sweet friend was acting out as much to keep Gracie distracted as she was because cursing was a large part of Tobi's vocabulary. How the woman's ass was going to survive long enough to break the habit was lost on Gracie.

JAX LEANED AGAINST the wall and listened to the discussion about increasing security around the Prairie Winds property but struggled to keep up because he was riveted by the woman shifting nervously on the sofa. Gracie had been lost in thought when Tobi had plopped down next to her, and Jax would have bet his entire inheritance that she'd been remembering last night. Her beautiful face had flushed and even from across the room he'd been able to see her eyes dilate. Watching the flush deepen and her breathing accelerate, he'd barely held back from throwing her over his shoulder and taking her right back to their bed.

When Gracie had tuned in to the discussion about her mother and brother she'd visibly paled and started fidgeting but Tobi had managed to curse enough to earn herself a couple of punishments, but she'd also managed to distract Gracie. Jax didn't doubt for a minute that his little pal would get her ass paddled, but he was sure her husbands knew exactly what the imp had been up to. Jax made a mental note to thank Tobi, he was grateful Gracie had such a sweet friend. At Kyle's nod, Kent pulled Tobi to her feet and led her to another chair and Jax sat next to Gracie. He took her hand in his and spoke quietly, *"Cariña,* we need you to tell the team everything you can remember about Raphael Baldamino, his estate, and anyone who worked for him. Can you do that?"

Jax listened with pride as she gave a detailed description of each person she'd interacted with while she'd been locked away in Baldamino's estate. Even though it was obvious she was uncomfortable with the discussion, she pushed through her fear and spoken calmly despite the death grip she had on his hands. He pried her hands open and began massaging circles in her palms and smiled as the muscles in her shoulders seemed to relax. Her insight about the people the man had surrounded her with had been impressive, particularly considering how young she'd been at the time. Gracie had also given them enough detail about the estate that it would be easy to locate on the Sat images their government contacts would provide.

She'd been speaking for several minutes when he felt a tremor move through her. When he asked her about it she'd gone completely still, hell, he didn't even think she had taken a breath for several seconds. Her voice had gone soft and the haunted look in her eyes told him what she was about to say was something she'd just remembered. "I don't know why I hadn't thought of this sooner, and…maybe it isn't important, it was actually only a rumor I heard from the staff."

When she stopped speaking, they all waited for her to gather her thoughts, and it was Kyle West who finally broke the silence, "Gracie, every detail is important. Please don't hesitate to tell us anything and everything you remember. There is no such thing as too much information when it comes to the safety and security of those we love, wouldn't you agree?"

Jax barely managed to suppress his smile, because Kyle had so blatantly hit Gracie in her most vulnerable spot. She was a true submissive because her deep desire to please, serve, and protect those she cared about was at the core of her personality. *This* was the side of Kyle West that Jax had seen so many times when they were SEALs. This was the team leader that had earned the respect of each man he'd worked with. And this was the Dom that every sub at the club knew to obey without question. The only submissive who had ever challenged Kyle was his wife.

―――

TOBI SAT ON Kent's lap and listened as her friend dispassionately described the people who had held her captive for months and the beautiful home and grounds that had served as little more than a prison. Gracie had also told them about the rumors she'd hear regarding other women being held in the compound. She'd never seen them, but had seen vans with dark tinted windows coming and going several times. Tobi wondered how Gracie was able to depersonalize the experience because she sounded almost like she'd been talking about someone else's experience.

Glancing up, she noticed Dan Deal leaning against a bookcase off to the side watching Gracie intently. Knowing that Dan was not only a club member, but also a well-respected psychologist, Tobi felt sure he was here to help Gracie if needed. Turning, she whispered in Kent's ear, "You brought Dan in to help Gracie, didn't you?" When he gave a quick nod she hugged him tight. Her eyes filled with unshed tears and she brushed her lips over his cheek as she spoke, "You and Kyle are the sweetest men ever, you know that?"

"Sweetness, you're pretty special yourself. And just so we're clear, we know why you were cursing earlier. Your attempts to distract your worried friend were admirable, and the only swats you'll be getting will be erotic. As long as you quit while you're ahead, that is." His soft chuckle vibrated through her and she sent up another prayer of thanks for the gifts she'd been given. Tobi laid her cheek against his shoulder and just let his warmth surround her as she tried to block out her own traumatic memories.

Despite her attempts to stay in the moment, Tobi's mind slowly moved back to the dark time in her life when she'd been her father's target during his drunken rages. Being bound to large nails in the walls while he'd beaten her had left her with enough emotional scars to last a lifetime. Kent and Kyle had helped her work through many of the triggers and she still talked to Dan on occasion, but overall she felt as if the weight of the world had been lifted from her shoulders. She'd even lost weight now that her self-image wasn't tied to her dad and brother's criticism.

After her brother's wife had tried to kill her and her sweet mother-in-law, the public relations smear her politically connected brother mounted had been a work of shear genius, even if it was completely misguided. She and her brother had only recently resumed speaking on the phone, but Tobi knew things would never be the same between them. Kent had obviously sensed her unhappiness because he'd shifted her so he could kiss the sensitive spot behind her ear. "Sweetness, I don't know where you've been, but I want you to come back to me. Those sounds of sadness have no place in your life now, baby." *Boy, truer words were never spoken, my love.*

Tobi smiled at him and whispered her thanks as she wondered what she and Gracie could do that would be fun, but wouldn't involve them leaving Prairie Winds. Deciding that a picnic down at the dock would be fun, she started working out all the details in her mind as the meeting wound down. The jet skis were still out and it would be fun to have one last blow out before everything was put up for the winter. They wouldn't get the really harsh weather that other parts of Texas often experienced, but it would certainly be too cold to play in the water soon enough. By the time the meeting was over, Tobi had a plan in mind and it was just a matter of getting her friends on-board for a bit of stress relief and fun.

Chapter Thirteen

REGI IMMERSED HERSELF in her work to the point Tank was giving her questioning glances. She and Tank had become fast friends when they'd begun working together a few years ago, he'd become a "stand-in big brother", fixing her kitchen faucet, taking care of her when she'd been ill, and teaching her to play poker. Even though Tank wasn't into the BDSM lifestyle, he was the most nonjudgmental person Regi had ever met. She felt guilty for snipping at him and hated how sharp her barked "What?" had sounded the last time she'd caught him looking at her as if she'd sprouted horns. She was skirting perilously close to an emotional edge and the hell of it was that she wasn't even sure why.

"Nothin', Reg. I was just wondering what crawled up your ass tonight, that's all. You've been snip-snapping at everybody since you got here today and that ain't like you at all." If he'd been indignant or belligerent, Regi would have whipped out one of her usual barbs, but the fact he'd actually sounded worried and a bit hurt sent feelings of guilt bubbling to the top, and she suddenly found herself fighting back tears. The sad truth was that she didn't know what had set her off today…at least she didn't know specifically what had triggered today's emotional firestorm, but it had been brewing for a while.

Just as she opened her mouth to apologize a deep voice

rumbled just over her left shoulder, "I know exactly what she needs, don't I, pet?" Regi froze. She hadn't been expecting either of the good docs this evening and a part of her wondered if that wasn't part of her edginess. Kirk Evans was six feet two inches of pure male temptation wrapped in a warrior's body. His dark complexion and hair were testaments to a heritage of Native American lineage that appeared to have gifted one man with all its best traits. What she'd been told, he and his medical practice partner had been friends since childhood and it had been the death of Brian Bennett's sister while giving birth that had prompted both men to specialize in the care of women. From bits and pieces she'd picked up over the past couple of years, both men had been in medical school when she and her child had died because of undiagnosed problems and they'd made it their personal mission to help other families avoid the same pitfalls.

Regi had been unable to stop the whole body shudder that pulsed through her when Kirk's words moved like a warm, moist breeze over the sensitive shell of her ear. She felt her sex flood and clench despite her intention to steer clear of the two Doms she was scared would be everything she couldn't ever have, it seemed her body had different ideas.

Brian Bennett whispered, "I can smell your arousal, darlin', so don't even try to deny it," against her right ear just before he used his tongue to trace its shell. Regi worried her knees were going to fold and placed her hand against the counter to steady herself. She hadn't even realized she'd closed her eyes until they fluttered open and she saw her boss, Kyle West, standing in front of her with his arms crossed over his chest looking at her as if he was studying and measuring her reactions.

When she jerked under his perusal, his sharp, "Stop," made her freeze instantly. Kyle nor Kent used their Dom personas with her often, but when they did, it was damned effective. Kyle didn't say anything for several seconds, he just watched her with the single-minded focus of a predator sizing up its prey. Regi could feel her heart beating frantically under his watchful gaze and she suddenly had a deeper respect for her bosses' sweet wife. She and Tobi West had become fast friends when the blonde bombshell stole the owners of the Prairie Winds Club hearts several months ago. Being the focus of Kyle West's attention when he was in full-on Dom mode was disconcerting as hell.

Regi had always dreamed of finding a Dom who would be strong enough to make her give up the control she held on to so tightly. And even though she respected her bosses and knew they were both fully capable of earning her submission, none of them had ever felt that way about the others. Their relationship had moved quickly from co-workers to friends and she was grateful none of them had been foolish enough to try to push the relationship in another direction.

Both Kyle and Kent had talked to her a number of times about what they felt she needed in a Dom, they hadn't always agreed, but Regi knew they would always have her best interests at heart. Their biggest points of contention were the men standing behind her. The simple truth was, the docs scared Regi to death. Not that she believed they'd ever hurt her physically...but they'd steal her heart, and Regi was terrified of the heartache that would follow when they found out she wasn't at all what they believed her to be.

In her peripheral vision, Regi had seen Brian and Kirk hand their membership cards to Tank. He'd quickly run them through the e-scanner logging them into the club, but she could feel them still standing behind her. Fearing that she was standing with her mouth gaping open looking like a fool, Regi finally managed to blink and bring her thoughts back to the moment. Obviously Kyle had sensed her return to the present because he smiled and nodded as if to acknowledge she'd returned her attention to him. His head tilted to the side ever so slightly and she could sense how closely he was considering his words. "Do you trust me, Regi?" When she nodded, he simply raised his brow and waited.

"Yes, Sir." She had always addressed Kyle and Kent as either Sir or Master whenever the club was open, and she knew they had both appreciated her respect for their positions as club owners and Doms.

Nodding once, he simply said, "If you three would come with me, please." He turned and headed down the short hallway to the office he and Kent shared. Regi followed, but her mind was racing and she wasn't sure if it was with fear or anticipation.

Kyle West had gone to the club's front entrance because two different club members had expressed their concern about Regi's unusual behavior. Knowing that her surliness was completely out of character had worried him and he'd made his way quickly in hopes of finding out what was troubling her. Just as he'd stepped into the foyer, he'd heard her exchange with Tank. The lines of emotional pain etching her sweet face tore at his heart. She was obviously struggling and there was only one way Kyle knew to get a wickedly bright submissive out of her head. And as luck would have it, the dynamic duo at the top of his "go to" list for this was already present and accounted for.

Kyle and Kent West knew most, if not all, of Regi's secrets, but she wasn't aware of that. They'd never told her everything they'd learned from the investigation they'd done after red flags had come up in her background check. Micah was their chief of security and when he'd pointed out discrepancies in the initial background, they had almost not hired her. But they'd made a few calls to former military contacts who had delved deeper and after meeting her face to face, they hadn't hesitated. He and Kent had only shared the details with Micah. The rest of the team had been given the "need to know" version. They'd planned to let her work through things as best she could, but she'd obviously hit some kind of emotional cross-over point and in desperate need of a respite from her demons.

When Brian Bennett and Kirk Evans first expressed an interest in Regi, he and Kent had been nervous about their intensity overwhelming the tiny woman they'd mistakenly seen as fragile. It had quickly become evident Regina Turner was a force to be reckoned with. The fact that she and Tobi were alike in so many ways helped them open their eyes to Regi's inner strength, and he hoped like hell he wasn't venturing too far out on that perception with what he was planning to do.

Chapter Fourteen

Brian Bennett had stepped into the club's large entry just in time to hear Regina Turner's guilt ridden response to her friend and co-worker, Tank. To his credit, Tank hadn't given them away and had just continued on as if Brian and Kirk hadn't entered the room. When most people would have chalked up Regi's outburst to a "bad day," he'd heard the underlying guilt in her voice and he knew there was something more important at stake.

He and Kirk had talked recently about the buildup they'd seen coming with Regi and they'd agreed that she was headed for a meltdown unless she found a way to release all the tension they'd seen building in her. Of course their discussion had quickly taken a major Segway into all the wicked ways they could provide her with that release. They'd laughed that it didn't seem to matter how old or how "professional" they were, it was always easy to slip back into that fun-loving frat-boy mentality.

They'd been introduced to the lifestyle during their freshman year of college by a couple of older fraternity brothers who had taken them to a club in Dallas. From that moment on, they'd both been hooked on the heady feeling of power they got from directing a woman's pleasure. Brian knew that his own pleasure fed off the woman he was topping, and even though he and Kirk had both topped women without the other, it was always much better when they worked together.

They'd both been strict sexual Dominants from the beginning, but their approach to punishments had changed after Beth died. His younger sister had been married to an asshole of the first order. When she'd become pregnant, he'd kept her from getting the prenatal care she'd needed because he preferred spending their money on his drug habit. By the time anyone in the family knew what was happening, she'd already gone into prenatal diabetic shock. Beth had slipped into a coma and died before he and Kirk had even gotten to the hospital. He knew he'd never forget hearing his mother's screams when the elevator doors slid open just outside the ICU where his sister had died just minutes before. That moment changed the entire course of not only his life, but that of his best friend as well.

By the time they'd settled in Kyle and Kent's office, Brian had managed to bring his thoughts back to the woman sitting between him and Kirk. She was clearly struggling and he was anxious to hear what Kyle had in mind.

KIRK EVANS SAT in the black leather wingback chair facing Kyle West's massive mahogany desk, watching and waiting. When he'd stood behind Regi out in the entryway, the tension was literally vibrating through her small body. His family had always given his Native American heritage the credit for his intuitive nature. As a kid, he'd been able to easily read the emotions of those around him and often could catch bits and pieces of their thoughts if everything was just right. All he'd gotten from Regi had been frustration and confusion, but now her uncertainty was quickly taking over.

As a trained submissive, Regi knew full well all three of them were monitoring her every response, and she was trying her damnedest to control each of her "tells." What she didn't realize was *that alone* was a huge tell. Kirk shifted his focus to Kyle, but kept Regi in his peripheral vision. His hope was that she'd relax a bit, but the tension radiating from her was soul deep, so his move hadn't seemed to make any difference.

Kyle West seemed to be studying all three of them with an intensity that Kirk had rarely seen him focus on anyone but his wife. There was no doubt that Tobi West was fully capable of keeping both of her husbands on their toes. He really was very fond of the little bundle of energy that had swept through the club much like the storm she'd seemed to emerge from, but he often wondered if she didn't still have some dragons left to slay as well.

Regi's body seemed to be winding tighter by the second and Kirk was beginning to think Kyle might have missed the window of opportunity he'd obviously been watching for. With every submissive, the time between perfectly off-balance and scared spitless was different, and one of the most important skills for a sexual Dominant was to be able to accurately judge that peak and exploit it. Catching a submissive at that precise moment was the gateway to reaching them on a soul deep level, and Kirk didn't doubt for a moment that was exactly what Kyle was watching for.

KYLE WAITED UNTIL he saw the subtle shift in the tilt of Regi's jaw that told him she was just about to bolt before he spoke. "Tell me what happened that had club members commenting on your attitude, sweetness." Kyle only called her by that name when he was acting as a Dominant and her boss, and he knew she hadn't missed the cue.

He watched as she opened her mouth to speak, but closed it again when she'd obviously reconsidered her response. *Smart girl.* Kyle watched as she took a deep, shuddering breath and looked up at him with tear-filled eyes, "I don't know." And then as if she'd thought he wouldn't believe her, she'd quickly added, "I really don't. My mind is just swimming and it's making me bitchy. I'm sorry, please don't fire me."

Kyle leaned back and hoped his expression hadn't shown how stunned he was that she'd think he might even consider firing her for having a bad day. *Jesus, Joseph, and Mary, am I that much of a tyrant to work for that she thinks I'd fire her because she is out of sorts?* Hell, this was the first time in years that he'd even known she was having a bad day. Damn, the woman hadn't ever missed a day of work that he was aware of and now that he considered it, that fact might well be part of her problem. She held herself to such a high performance standard it was unlikely anyone could keep it up forever, and she'd done it a lot longer than probably should have been expected. *Well, darlin', time to blow off a bit of steam.*

"I'll tell you what, I think you need a bit of down time, sweetness. But rather than sending you home, I'd like to offer you an alternative solution." He'd managed to hold back his smile at her wide-eyed look when he'd mentioned sending her home. For a dedicated worker and submissive, sending her away would be a harsh punishment, much too harsh for someone already struggling with feeling overwhelmed. He let her think for a few moments and then asked, "Are you open for suggestions?"

Her stammered, "Y-yes, Sir," was music to his ears.

"I want you to spend the evening with Masters Brian and Kirk. I want you to talk with them honestly. Negotiate a scene with them in one of the private rooms, because I don't believe any of the public areas are in your best interest this evening." Kyle knew Brian and Kirk would have noticed he hadn't asked Regi again if she trusted him, even though it was usually among the first questions Doms asked when getting ready to deliver unwelcome news to a sub. She'd shown her trust in the lobby when she'd followed him to the office, but the offer he'd just put on the table was going to require a much deeper trust, and all three Doms knew it. He didn't doubt for a minute that she trusted him as much as she could trust anyone, and right now he had the feeling she trusted herself the least of all.

Kyle saw her eyes widen in shock and heard her small gasp. She sprang up out of her chair, "Wait. You're turning me over to the Wacky-Doodle Doctor Duo?"

What the fuck was that supposed to mean? Besides the fact she is obviously spending too much time with my wife. Kyle hated that he'd been unsuccessful in suppressing his smile, but hell, he ought to have been damned impressed he hadn't laughed out loud.

"Sweetness, I'm fairly certain Master Brian and Master Kirk are going to make you pay dearly for that remark, as well they should. I'll remind you that as an employee of this club, you will treat all of its members with respect." He leaned forward placing his hands on his tented fingers drawing her full attention before continuing, "And speaking as a Dom to a club submissive, I'll remind you that there are consequences for being disrespectful, so I suggest you apologize quickly and sincerely."

Regi turned to both men and whispered, "Master Kyle is right. I shouldn't have said that out loud." Her tone was proper even if her words and posture screamed anything but remorse. Kyle also noticed that she hadn't actually apologized but had only said that she shouldn't have stated her opinion out loud, a glaring difference that he was certain neither Brian nor Kirk had missed. This evening was shaping up to be interesting indeed.

Chapter Fifteen

Tobi leaned back against the small sofa in the living room of Micah and Jax's home listening as Gracie and the other subs they'd invited giggled about the latest club gossip. The only one who seemed to be holding back was Regi, and she'd seemed to be strung awfully tight for the past couple of weeks. Tobi had heard via the club's grapevine that Regi had reluctantly scened with the good docs who had obviously been interested in her for a long time. But if the shadows under her friends eyes were any indication, the release they'd no doubt given her hadn't been enough to completely ease whatever shadows were chasing her.

Making a mental note to invite Regi to lunch sometime soon, Tobi turned back to the window and watched the pampas grass at the corner of the porch dancing in the breeze. It was a bit cooler today than it had been last week, proof that summer was drawing to a close, and she was grateful the club's annual end of summer pool party had been a few nights before. Finally returning her attention to her friends, her thoughts just seemed to tumble out in a jumbled up mess. "I think we should plan something special for our men. A sort of end of summer blowout. They are always doing stuff for…well and *to* us, and I'd like to take the reins for once. I think we should plan a picnic. We could start a barbeque then play a bit with the jet skis before settling down for dinner around the fire pit." When she noticed they were all staring at her, she asked, "What? Don't give me that look, I know it'll be cool out there, but we have the fire pits that EAG made. Damn I love those portable fireplaces. And crap on a cracker, the erotic scenes they cut into the sides are freaking spectacular at night." They all giggled at her and Tobi knew she'd gotten that faraway look of a woman remembering earthquake inducing sex. Shaking her head to clear it, she continued, "Did you know Clint and his crew made those metal tables in the gazebo? They can be plugged in and warmed up so they'll be nice and toasty when we're wet." The tables were amazing and Tobi had immediately understood what the men had been thinking about when they'd helped the staff at EAG Fabrication in Sealy design them.

When Gracie and the others started giggling, Tobi realized what she'd said and laughed. "You dip-shi...sh-ka-bobs, you know what I meant." She looked around the room and noticed the tiny camera on the top shelf and rolled her eyes. "Damn. Not only is it impossible to plan a dang surprise, but now I'll probably be in trouble for just walking in the same neighborhood as a curse word."

Shaking her head at her giggling friends, Tobi turned to Noelle Chambers. "Will you and Neal be able to come out Sunday?" Noelle was a fellow sub at the club but she was also a successful prosecutor in Austin and worked terrible hours, if you listened to her husband, Neal. Tobi had laughed when she'd learned that Neal was a pediatrician, because for a doctor to complain about the hours their spouse worked seemed like a pretty significant statement.

"Sure, I don't think either of us are on call and I'll bet your men have some interesting plans for those tables this winter. Seems only fair that we one-up them on the deal."

When Tobi had first come to Prairie Winds, she'd been the target of a couple of catty-jealous women. It had been Noelle who had come to her rescue in the club's lounge and they'd formed a tight friendship almost immediately. One of the women had been banned from almost all of the reputable BDSM clubs in the country and several overseas as a result of the report Kent and Kyle submitted to their network. She hadn't been banned for what she'd said, but for her refusal to be held accountable and the fact she'd only been pretending to be a sub to get closer to the bachelor West brothers. She'd intentionally set out to hurt Tobi in an effort to get her to walk away from Kent and Kyle. She'd also convinced another submissive to help her, but the other woman, Mary Dillon, had been truly remorseful for her part. Mary had accepted her punishment and had slowly worked her way back into everyone's good graces.

Kent and Kyle hadn't ever told Tobi how Mary had been punished but she'd heard from the other subs that it hadn't been pretty. Doms Ash Moore and Dex Raines had been the ones to punish Mary and Tobi knew they had reputations as harsh disciplinarians. Tobi had worried about the young sub until she'd seen her scene with them again several weeks later. Even though their scenes were much more intense than what Tobi would probably ever feel comfortable with, it seemed to work for the three of them, and that was all that mattered. Evidently, Mary discovered she was a bit of a pain slut, which seemed to work out well since both Ash and Dex were more than happy to meet her *edgier* needs.

"What about you, Mary?" Tobi asked.

"I don't have to work, but I'll have to check with Masters Ash and Dex. I'm still not allowed to participate in club activities without their permission." Tobi could see the remorse that still lingered in her expression and wished the young woman could forgive herself. Tobi knew that Ash and Dex were managing Mary's club time because they were concerned she'd inadvertently get herself in trouble again. Kent had explained that since Mary was a masochist she would need strong guidance until she learned her own limitations and boundaries. One of the things Mary had yet to fully understand was that once her punishment and suspension were over, the membership viewed the incident as over. It didn't mean she'd earned their trust again immediately, but she was definitely starting with a clean slate, that concept was actually one of Tobi's favorite parts of the lifestyle, so she hoped Mary was able to come to terms with it soon.

"Okay, well talk to them and as soon as you can, let me know what they say. What shall we make to eat?" The room went completely silent and Tobi glanced around at the gaping stares once again focused on her. "What? We can do this. How hard can it be to cook a few steaks on a grill? And potato salad and baked beans surely don't require a PhD."

Regi Turner, The Masters of the Prairie Winds Club's resident feisty receptionist-and-more, was the first to speak, "First of all, girlfriend, none of us can cook for shit and that alone is a warning flag as big as the AT&T Stadium. And if that isn't enough...not all of us have *men*. And don't be looking at me with those damned puppy dog eyes that work like magic on my bosses, because I'm immune to them, sweetie." She held up her hand to stop the protest Tobi was ready to speak, "And before you let that nonsense fly, let me remind you a couple of play dates do not mean those doctors are my men. Hell, they might not even be around by the weekend when they find out I have to move."

Tobi wasn't fooled by Regi's comments and doubted that Gracie or Noelle were fooled either. And right on cue Noelle Chambers leaned forward to snag her margarita off the low table in front of her. "I call bullshit, Regi. Everybody knows those two hottie docs are working their magic on you and don't even try throwing that BS in my direction. And you have to move because your roomie got married, it isn't like you're moving to the damned moon. You're just moving across town." Noelle had a mind and mouth as sharp as any Tobi had ever seen and she was in rare form tonight for some reason. "Shit, Regi, I don't know why you don't give them a chance, hell, they are gorgeous, professional, and genuinely nice guys. And if the scuttlebutt amongst the club's subs is as accurate as it usually is, they are both firm but fair Doms who know how to make the sub they are topping come eight ways to Sunday. Truthfully, from what I've seen, they are incredibly insightful, and I haven't seen them play with any sub since they set their sights on you."

Gracie leaned forward and set her drink down before looking over at Regi. "I don't want to get into your business, Regi, but I have to say the both of them are wicked nice if you know what I mean. Please invite them. If you do and they decline, then you'll know and these two will be off your case about it." She waved her hand in Tobi and Noelle's direction before continuing, "And if they do accept, you'll have a great evening with two wonderful men. Sounds like a win-win to me."

Tobi leaned back and tried to suppress her grin, because she knew her friend too well…this sales pitch was far from over. Gracie had a soft spot for both docs, but particularly for Brian Bennett. He'd been the one to treat her the night she'd arrived at Prairie Winds after being assaulted by the man who'd been stalking Tobi. Brian had been incredibly gentle and had even followed up with her several times in the weeks following the incident. Tobi knew that Gracie thought of him as a good friend, and they both also knew how much Brian and Kirk looked forward to the little time they got to spend with Regi.

For the first time since Tobi had known Regina Turner, she saw a chink in her spirited friend's armor. When Regi looked up, there were unshed tears in her eyes. "You know Kirk's parents own a big ranch not too far from here, right?" They all shook their heads and Regi's shoulders sagged. "Well, they do…a flippin' huge one. Enormous actually. And Brian's parents are in the oil business. Everything they do is covered by one media outlet or another." Tobi didn't like where she thought this conversation was headed because Regi's insecurities sounded much too familiar. "Then there's me…"

Yep, I knew it. Well if that doesn't beat all.

"Hold on a second. So you aren't trying to dish up some horseshit about them being better than you because their families have money, are you? Because I'm seriously gonna have to crawl right up your ass if that's the case. Remember that little friends and family speech you gave me the night Gracie arrived? Well, right back atcha, sister!" Tobi was in full "Regi-mode" by the time she'd finished speaking. All the members and staff at the club knew the term because Regi might be tiny, but she was a toe-tapping, hands-on-hips, snapping bolts of lightning goddess when crossed.

This time Regi was the target of everyone's attention and she looked anything but comfortable with the role.

After a huge sigh of resignation, she seemed to pull herself together. "Okay, I'll invite them. But don't think this is a done deal, girlfriends. Really, you just don't understand all the implications here."

Something in the back of Tobi's mind told her there was a lot of pain in Regi's background, but now wasn't the time to get into it. *Yep, definitely a girls' margarita lunch in our future.*

"Well, finally. Now, we need to plan the menu and decide on all the details. I really want to surprise the men and that is going to take a team effort in this place." Tobi grinned in victory. The entire Prairie Winds property was covered with surveillance equipment that would have the CIA and NSA drooling with envy, so keeping anything secret required strategic planning and enormous amounts of stealth. "Gracie, didn't you say something about Jax's sister visiting around Labor Day?"

"Yes, Elza will be here so I'd like to invite someone for her to spend time with, but I don't know anyone who signs." One of the first things Jax and Gracie had discovered they had in common was the fact they both had younger siblings who were deaf. "Do any of you know of someone? I'm not trying to fix her up, but I want her to feel included. And I'm only comfortable inviting someone that one of us knows personally." Tobi grinned because if Elza thought her brother and Micah were protective, she hadn't seen anything yet. Tobi had seen Gracie in "protective mode" and it was something to behold.

Regi looked up and grinned, "Tank signs." All three women gapped at her. "What? He does...really. He told me that when he was growing up they had a neighbor whose young son was profoundly hearing impaired and he didn't like that the little boy often sat to the side alone at their neighborhood functions, so he learned to sign so he could interact with him. They are still close to this day as I understand it." Regi grinned as she stood up, "I have to head up to the club and get things ready for this weekend. Let me know what I need to do for the party, besides make nice with the good fanny docs." She left the others shaking their heads at her jab at the doctors who they all believed would be so good for her.

Tobi couldn't hold back her laughter at Regi's outrageousness. "Just when I thought the lot of you couldn't surprise me anymore, one of you pulls this sort of thing out of your ass...embled knowledge." Tobi giggled and then said, "Come on, let's go outside. I know just the place where we can plan our surprise without being overheard."

Chapter Sixteen

KYLE GLARED AT the screen before turning to Micah asking, "Is she serious? Is there a place outside where we can't hear them?" He didn't think they'd missed anything vital, but his wife was very resourceful so he wouldn't be surprised to learn she'd found a corner for her pow-wow. And in all honesty, it didn't really matter because they weren't up to anything other than party planning, but she had essentially issued a challenge to her Masters and the entire security team, so now it was game on.

Micah scowled at the array of screens in front of him and began using a joystick to track the women as they walked to the boathouse. "They all need to be beaten more, you know that, right? And tell your dads the same thing because this has Lilly West written all over it." Kent and Kyle's mother was a force of nature. No one doubted that she was a sub in the bedroom, but in every other venue she was hell on wheels.

Kyle had just opened his mouth to question his friend when he heard Tobi explain to the others how his mom had shown her the one spot they'd be able to speak freely. He'd heard himself growl in frustration before asking Micah, "How did you know?"

Micah laughed, "I saw them yesterday just wandering through the gardens as I was coming up to the main house.

They were idly chatting but paused as they met me and Tobi turned absolutely crimson. Damn I love that trait, makes her so much easier to read. Grace's darker coloring allows her to hide a blush easier. You and Kent are lucky bastards on that point." Kyle knew his friend was trying to get him to lighten up, but it wasn't really working. He didn't know exactly why he was so frustrated. Admittedly, he had never liked being challenged, this was something more, and Kyle wasn't sure exactly what else had burrowed beneath his skin. Kyle felt his instincts begin to kick in and he'd learned long ago to never ignore the sixth sense that all Special Forces operatives stake their lives on each and every day. "I'm worried we've got a point of vulnerability, if there is a place the women can talk without us hearing them, then there is a place where Baldamino has access." The hair on the back of Kyle's neck was standing up and that was always a sign that he needed to sit up and pay very close attention.

Micah nodded, "I watched the tapes last night to find out exactly where your mom and Tobi went. Jax and I checked it out early this morning and there is a narrow dead spot down by the dock, and of course we won't be able to hear anything if they go swimming." Micah must have sent a text to Jax and Kent because Kyle saw both men jogging down separate paths toward the boathouse.

They watched as the women made their way out to the end of the dock. The four of them spent several minutes huddled together in conversation as they cast nervous glances around them. *Yeah, you know you're in it deep, sweet subs. Just keep digging.* Kyle watched Tobi's failed attempts to look nonchalant as she pointed toward the jet skis tied alongside the edge of the dock. It was obvious the other women weren't convinced that whatever Tobi's suggestion had been was a good idea. But when she'd pointed to a boat in the middle of the river Kyle had groaned, "Fuck, is that my dads' boat?" Before Micah could answer, Kyle saw his mom standing on the small elevated bridge waving like a wild woman. Once the other women saw her, Noelle waved back and the others quickly followed suite. *I am going to paddle Tobi's ass so hard she is going to be sitting on a fucking pillow for a month of Sundays.*

They watched the monitors helplessly as the women grabbed life jackets and put them on quickly. They'd just fired up the skis when Jax and Kent started down the docks wooden planking. "You know they've seen Jax and Kent. But they are going to swear they didn't. Goddammit to hell, she isn't going to be able to sit until Thanksgiving." Kyle had to force himself to watch as they took off at full throttle. Both he and Kent had thought the toys were a bit too tame, and now their decision to have the engines jacked-up seemed like a very bad idea, because they really were too much for Tobi and Noelle to handle. Both drivers had nearly lost their passengers when they'd taken off from the dock. It they didn't manage to kill themselves it was going to be a miracle.

"You know, they'd all earned a paddling even before they hijacked the jet skis, but I think maybe we can use this to our advantage." Micah's tone had a pure Dom-evil thread running through it, and Kyle hoped his forced chuckle didn't sound as hollow as it felt. He'd known the man for too many years to miss the sound of his friend's mind spinning so Kyle could only hope he was coming up with something appropriately sinister. After all, Micah Drake had been called "Hannibal" more than once for his ability to "pull a plan together" almost out of thin air.

Jax stood alongside Kent watching as the women took off on the souped-up watercraft. He'd nearly popped a vein when Gracie had almost been flipped off the back as Tobi had nailed it. Tobi had sprayed both he and Kent with stale smelling water in the process, and Jax saw Kent's face turn a brilliant crimson. Swiping his hand over his face to clean off the river water, Kent had literally growled, "She is still gonna be sittin' on a pillow come Christmas morning, I swear it."

When his phone vibrated in his pocket, Jax knew without even looking who was on the other end. "You better have a plan because right now I'm too mad at all of them to even think about touching them."

"Working on it. But right now, I'm more concerned about them misjudging and doing a header into Kent and Kyle's parents' boat in the middle of the river. That is their sweet mother standing out there waving the women on. But my biggest concern is the fact we have incoming from the west." Jax immediately focused on the boat that was coming up the river much too fast to be fishing or pleasure cruising. Kent had followed his line of gaze and instinctively taken off toward the small speedboat tied at the other end of the dock.

Jax untied the lines while Kent started the motor. Even though it had only taken them a few seconds, it didn't take Jax long to calculate the speed and trajectory and know they weren't going to make it in time. Kent hit the horn and Jax saw Tobi's jet ski slow marginally and he assumed she knew better than to try to out run them. But as she'd turned back around Jax could tell she'd seen the boat coming up on them because she'd waved off Noelle and Mary. *Good girl, split up. Let's make sure we know what we're dealing with.*

When the boat didn't change course to follow Noelle and Mary, Jax felt his breath leave his chest in a whoosh. Tobi appeared to be shouting instructions over her shoulder at Gracie. Jax could see Gracie tighten her arms around Tobi and she leaned perfectly as Tobi went into a sharp banking curve around the Wests' boat sitting almost dead center in the middle of the river. As they got closer, Jax heard Kent cursing, "Holy fucking hell, that's mom. What the—" he'd just barely caught a glint of sunlight reflecting off the scope of a weapon before the rest of his words were drowned out by the booming sounds of gunfire.

"Holy shit. What is she shooting? A fucking cannon?" Jax couldn't completely suppress the awe from his voice.

"Don't encourage her for God's sake. Why the dads let her spend so much time at the range is a mystery that ranks right up there with where Jimmy Hoffa is buried." Kent had circled sharply to the right to avoid getting shot by his own mother. The men fishing in small boats along the bank yelled in frustration when they'd nearly been rolled by the wake Kent sent their way. The next volley of shots from Lilly West must have hit their mark because the speedboat appeared to have lost control and was headed for the rock bank on the other side of the river. Just as Kent headed that way the boat caught fire and exploded sending smoke billowing into the air. *Well fuck! So much for finding out the whos and whys of this cluster.*

⁓

TOBI AND GRACIE had scrambled onto the boat with Lilly

just as the boat that had been chasing them blew into a thousand pieces. They both turned their faces from the horror because even though Tobi wasn't an expert on explosions, she knew the boat wouldn't have had enough fuel on board to cause an explosion that large. Whoever had been on that boat had obviously been well armed and knowing they'd been chasing her and Gracie sent chills up Tobi's spine.

Lilly lowered the gun from her shoulder and sighed. "Well, shit...my husbands are gonna be really pissed off about this. And I can't even imagine how mad my sons will be. They tend to overreact to things like this." She turned to Tobi then pointed to her phone. "See? Thirty-two missed calls in seven minutes. I do believe that's a record." She grinned before looking up and then sobering. "Incoming."

Tobi looked up into the fire-shooting eyes of the calmer of her two husbands. *Oh shit!*

Chapter Seventeen

Parker Andrews leaned against the back wall of the observation room situated alongside the conference room and watched as Tobi West and Grace Santos answered the same questions for the fifth time. The women had been doing great, but their men were getting restless. Pushing away from the wall, he said, "Come on, let's go get some coffee. They'll keep the women safely corralled until we get back." Noelle and Mary had already been released because they hadn't seen much since they'd already rounded a large bend in the river before all hell had broken loose.

"Where's our mother?" Now that Kyle's voice had lost its deadly sneer, Parker was more inclined to answer. Even though this wasn't Parker's jurisdiction, he was sticking around to help his friends navigate the system and to keep the Doms from all landing in jail for interfering in an ongoing investigation. When the four men had first arrived, he'd actually heard one of the deputies working the case mention keeping the women in protective custody so they wouldn't have to deal with their men.

"There is another conference room down the hall. She is being interviewed separately since she is the one who fired the weapon. And just out of curiosity, where did she get that fucking gun anyway. Damn, guys, you need to talk to your dads about what they put in her hands. Christ almighty that woman was loaded for bear and she is a damned good shot, too. Hell, she drilled the motor—deliberately from what I heard. She wanted to disable the boat. Well mission accomplished, holy shit. Unfortunately, the kill shot for the motor went into their weapons stash." The information on the men's boat was being withheld from the media for the time being, but the fact Lilly West had taken out two well-known enforcers for a Latin American drug lord was going to make her a folk hero in most law enforcement circles. And the fact that she was the beautiful wife of two of Texas's wealthiest businessmen was only going to add fuel to the fire. *Talk about a shit storm in the making.* If Parker had to guess, he'd put his money on there being at least two songs about her by the end of the year.

"Your dads are down there and, of course, their team of lawyers is flanking her as well. But honestly, it's really not going to be an issue. She was clearly defending her daughter-in-law from an obvious threat, so it's a no-brainer that she'll be leaving here tonight free and clear. I can tell you the D.A. isn't going to touch this one. Particularly when Noelle is backing up her story about warning them away to safety." They all grabbed drinks and made their way to a small table outside the ground floor cafeteria. Once they'd all sat down, Parker continued, "We got lucky and got the numbers on the boat from your security footage." Turning to Micah, Parker nodded his thanks. "They aren't going to release this just yet, but here's the scoop on the guys in the boat."

Micah sat in stunned silence as Parker gave them background information on the two men who had been killed in the explosion. They'd been identified by security cameras located at the small marina up river where they'd picked up the boat. Obviously they hadn't expected the small mom and pop operation to have any security equipment because they'd used the same boat for several days and had never made any attempt to conceal their identities. Knowing two killers had been watching the Prairie Winds property waiting for an opportunity to get to Gracie made Micah's stomach pitch.

These were men who made a living killing others and the thought they'd gotten too close to Gracie and Tobi this afternoon sent an electric current of fear straight up his spine. Parker had told them the two were the go-to guys for anyone with cash in-hand, but their Central American connections were well documented. The more Parker had told them, the deeper Micah sank into operative mode and just the briefest glance at Jax showed he was following a similar path. Kyle West listened intently and when Parker had finished, he'd nodded once and then turned to the others. "I'd like you to send out messages to some of our other team members. And I'd like to bring in a few more if no one has any objections. We can use the extra manpower on this and several of our former teammates have expressed an interest in joining if they can find work around here."

This was news to Micah and he was anxious to talk to the Wests to find out who Kyle was talking about. Parker cleared his throat and leaned forward, "We're hiring and I'm sure the county's force is looking as well. I doubt the money is appealing, but it would be a start for them." They all four nodded because it was well known that Texans had a real fondness for hiring veterans so anyone they sent that way would likely be hired immediately. Parker hadn't leaned back and relaxed so Micah knew he had more to say. "Listen, if you guys want to leave here today with your subs, you need to lighten up. There was scuttlebutt earlier about putting Tobi and Gracie in protective custody because you were going all 'Alpha' on them." Micah would have laughed out loud at the sight of the Police Captain using air quotes…that is, if he hadn't been so stunned by what Parker had just said.

Looking at his friends, Micah saw similar shocked expressions. Jax recovered first, "Seriously? They think we'd hurt our women? What they hell. Where does that bullshit come from?"

"Listen, I'm a Dom so I understand what's going through your head when you make comments about paddling their asses for putting themselves in danger. However not everybody around here *gets it* so you need to back off. And this place has cameras everywhere, that's why we're out here. This was one of the few places I knew I'd be able to speak freely." Parker shook his head and laughed, "Jesus, guys, lighten the fuck up. You all looked like I just kicked your puppy. The girls should be done soon, let's get back in there.

Walking back down the hall, Micah noticed the furtive glances they were receiving from officers they met along the way and he wondered if they had really acted inappropriately enough to warrant the disdained looks they were getting. Rounding the corner to see Gracie and Tobi sitting on a bench with tear-streaked faces while the legal eagles the Wests had called in hovered nearby was all the explanation he needed. When Gracie looked up and grimaced he wanted to kick himself. Opening his arms to her, his knees almost buckled in relief when she scrambled to her feet and ran into his embrace.

Chapter Eighteen

IT HAD BEEN a week since the river incident and all the guys were still peeved, but Gracie had noticed that Tobi was finally able to sit down without wincing. She'd gotten her own paddling but there wasn't any doubt that Tobi had borne the brunt of the blame. Gracie hadn't seen Lilly since that day and wondered what had happened on her end. Tobi had assured her that Lilly was capable of "handling" her men, but Gracie wasn't so sure. It seemed to her that Kent and Kyle had surely learned some of their tricks from their dads, so likely things at the elder Wests' home were tense as well.

Tobi had called earlier and mentioned bringing lunch down to the Forum Shops, so Gracie had hurried to finish up her work so they could enjoy their lunch. Gracie loved the white gazebo overlooking the river, and sitting there today gazing over the slow moving water was calming. But even though the atmosphere was peaceful, it was obvious there was something on Tobi's mind. Gracie finally got tired of waiting for her friend to talk, so she turned to her and left no room for argument when she said, "Spit it out, sister." Sighing to herself at Tobi's attempt at looking contrite, she continued, "I know something is bothering you, because you are much too quiet. And you have that look that tells me you have already done some-thing…something you don't think I'm going to like. So out with it."

Tobi stared out over the water for several minutes before taking a deep breath and squaring her shoulders. "Okay. I helped the guys send your mom and brother to Sealy to stay with the Bollingers." Gracie came out of her seat like a shot, but as soon as she opened her mouth to speak, Tobi raised her hand to stop her. "Listen for a minute. Both of them are vets, their kids are older, all of them know their way around weapons, and they don't have any connection to you whatsoever. They are also hunters so they have plenty of firepower at their disposal. Jax's family has already sent a security firm out to install a state of the art security system, which isn't costing them anything."

Gracie collapsed back into her seat and didn't even try to hold back the tears. A part of her mind knew that moving her mom and brother was the right thing to do. But another part of her wanted to fight this to the end because no one had even consulted her. She was tired of being at the whim of whatever direction fate's winds decided to blow. First she'd had to cope with the loss of her father, then the disaster with Baldamino followed by years of living in fear, and now the battle was even more in the forefront because he'd found her.

When would it end? There were a hundred ways this could go and ninety-nine of them ended badly. Gracie was both physically and emotionally drained. She'd been covering up the fact that she was dropping weight but that wasn't going to last much longer. Jax had already looked at her with a raised eyebrow earlier today when he'd spanned her waist with his hands. He'd leaned down and whispered in her ear, promising they would be having a discussion later, and that wasn't likely going to be a walk in the park either.

Gracie finally found her focus and turned to Tobi, "Why you? I mean, why are you telling me and not Micah or Jax? I don't understand. And why didn't my mom call? And Alex should have at least texted me. I'm just so tired of not having any power in my life. Everything has been out of control since the night they dragged my dad out of our home. And every time I think I'm getting my feet under me, someone yanks on the damned rug again and I go tumbling down a steep flight of stairs into chaos." By the time she'd finished, she was hiccupping her sobs as the tension just seemed to flow from her.

While she'd been blustering and blubbering, Tobi had moved so she was now sitting alongside Gracie. She'd draped her arm over Gracie's shaking shoulders and just let her cry for several minutes. Once the sobs had started to diminish, Tobi used one of the linen napkins from their picnic to dry Gracie's tears before answering, "I asked to be the one to tell you, because I was the one to suggest the move and the location. Your mom understood the importance of not contacting you because your phone was already being pinged by someone in Central America. Please don't be mad at us, we really were trying to help."

Gracie felt sorry for her friend and turned to hug her. "I know and I'm sorry for venting to you. It's just that I had such high hopes when I got this job. It was the answer to so many prayers that I thought this time things were going to be different. But now my mom and brother are forced to hide with strangers and I'm basically a prisoner again. Don't get me wrong...I love it here, but just knowing that I can't even drive into town to shop or to go out for a burger...well, it makes me want to go all that much more."

They sat together in silence for several more minutes

before Gracie saw a flicker of light across the river. It was a reflection of light from the trees and she froze. "Did you see that?"

⁓

JAX PRESSED ON the earpiece as he made his way toward the gazebo where Gracie and Tobi had been eating lunch. He and Micah had promised to leave it to Tobi, and had agreed to only monitor their conversation. And he'd kept his end of the bargain until her crying had completely unhinged him, and then he'd begun making his way toward her. Grabbing a com unit had been a last minute decision and now he was grateful he'd taken the time. When he'd heard Gracie tell Tobi about the reflection of light he'd taken off running. He knew Micah would be sending out the word but if someone was on the other side of the river with a scope, there was no way they'd ever get there in time to catch whoever it was.

His height had been a disadvantage so many times during his time in the Special Forces that Jax had often caught himself cursing it, but today he was grateful for his longer than normal stride. Just as he made his way into the gazebo he saw a flash across the river. Launching himself at the women, he circled his arms around both of them and rolled to the ground. The first shot had been so close he'd felt the air rush past his left ear. He rolled under the steel tables just as a second bullet pinged off the curved leg of the steel leg of the unit.

Jax heard the jet skis and speedboat roar to life down at the dock a split second before the third bullet took out a chunk of the concrete floor near his head. "Stay down, but start scooting toward the edge. As soon as you are close, roll quickly over the edge and then run like hell into the trees. Kent and Kyle are on their way down from the main house and we've already sent men to the other side, although I don't think there is much hope they can catch him, it might at least make him divide his attention and buy us a few seconds." He was grateful both women nodded quickly and then simply followed his instructions without asking any questions.

Both of them managed to roll over the edge of the gazebo's concrete floor into the floor bed and then scamper into the trees without any more shots being fired their way. Which Jax knew meant one of two things, either the shooter had heard the watercraft and abandoned his objective in favor of escape or his sights had actually been set on Jax. He'd stayed down for just a few seconds before he'd followed them into the relative safety of the trees.

Out of the hundreds of close calls Jax had experienced while a part of the Special Forces teams, the incident today had totally eclipsed everything else he'd experienced. The fear that had lanced through him when he realized the danger Gracie and Tobi were in had almost frozen him. If he hadn't been flooded with adrenaline as they made their way back to the main house with Kent and Kyle, he might had been a bit more introspective about the significance of his reaction. But every step he'd taken had sent a caveman's pounding need to protect his woman surging through his blood. By the time they reached the back door his body language must have been entirely too clear because Kent had pulled him aside. "Are you going to be okay? Because I'm gonna level with you, man, you look like you need to work off the spin before you say or do something you'll regret later."

One of the things being a SEAL had taught Jax was that

coming down from what they called a mission high was often more difficult than the mission itself. He'd heard many tales about colleagues unintentionally hurting others during those first few hours simply because their bodies were trained to deal with the adrenaline rush for a longer period of time, so the decline was often a much longer process for a returning soldier.

Running his hand through his hair in a move he knew conveyed the raw edge of emotion he was walking, he shook his head. "Honestly? I don't know. I've never been so damned scared in my entire life. Knowing Gracie and Tobi were in danger felt like someone sticking swords through my heart. And here's the kicker, I don't even think the shooter was aiming at them. I think I was the target."

Kyle had moved ahead with the women and Jax hadn't realized that Gracie had doubled back until after he'd spoken. When he looked up and saw her standing just behind Kent's left shoulder, his heart sank. He watched as all the color drained from her face and her eyes filled with terror. The look of absolute horror on her beautiful face made him wish he could pull the words back, but of course he couldn't. And her whispered words, "He'll kill you just because I love you…it's all the reason he'll need." The anguish in her voice tore at his heart. Kent heard her and must have recognized the desperation, because he turned just as her knees folded, catching her in his arms.

Chapter Nineteen

MICAH SAT IN front of the fireplace staring at the dying embers and wondered how things had gotten so screwed up in just a matter of hours. As SEALs, they'd have termed it FUBAR, fucked up beyond all recognition. But it didn't matter what label you slapped on it, everything was still spinning wildly out of control. Once Grace had come to, she'd been adamant about leaving Prairie Winds to the point that she and Tobi had actually ended up yelling at one another.

Kyle West had finally sent his nearly hysterical wife upstairs with Kent with promises of a sound spanking for her interference. Each time Kyle had tried to rationalize with Gracie, his tiny tigress of a wife had jumped in the middle of their discussion and the hell of it was, her points had been valid. But Tobi's refusal to stay quiet had pushed her husband over an edge and Micah wasn't sure he'd ever seen his friend that angry before today. He wasn't entirely sure Tobi hadn't been intentionally trying to antagonize Kyle in order to deflect Gracie's attention. If it had been her plan, she'd failed miserably.

As Kent had carried her out of the room over his shoulder, Tobi had still been cursing a blue streak about Neanderthals and Doms with God complexes and how good Kyle would look with his paddle stuck up his ass like a popsicle stick. It was the only time Micah had seen even a flicker of emotion cross Gracie's face and it had been easy to see she was trying valiantly to suppress her smile.

Rubbing his hand over the stubble on his chin, Micah moved his gaze from the fire and looked over at Jax and sighed. "I really don't know what to do. Her expression was so blank when we left Kyle's office. The complete lack of emotion tells me that we didn't reach her tonight and I honestly just don't know how to do it. I've never seen someone build a wall around themselves so quickly or effectively. She honestly thinks she is protecting us by leaving."

This time it was Jax who leaned forward with his arms resting on his knees and stared into the dying fire as he shook his head. "I'll never forgive myself for letting her hear my words. Whoever was shooting wasn't trying to kill me, just scare me off. And I agree that it tells us they want her alive, and that it doesn't seem as though they know who we are or they'd have known better than to just take pot shots." Although the truth of it was that most soldiers in Central America were only loyal to whoever was currently in power or who had the highest cash offer. Even if they knew he was a soldier, it was likely whoever had hired the shooter honestly didn't understand the honor code American soldiers lived by or they'd have given his life for either Gracie or Tobi and never had to think twice about the decision.

Short of holding her against her will, Micah wasn't sure how long they were going to be able to keep her at the compound. After Tobi was gone, Kyle had continued talking to Gracie because she had flatly refused to even respond to either he or Jax. It had finally gotten late enough in the afternoon that she had agreed to rest before taking off under the cover of darkness. Just as Micah started to respond to Jax, there was a knock on their door.

Jax moved to their front door and when he opened it, Lilly West swept into the room like the tornado she often proved to be. Both of her husbands were trailing along behind her, but neither Dean nor Dell West seemed as agitated as their lovely wife. She looked around the room before turning to Micah. "Where is she? We're putting a stop to this nonsense right now. Thinking I spent all those hours answering those inane questions at the law enforcement center just so she can waltz out of here big as she pleases. I don't think so...no siree." Her voice had trailed off but he could see it was only going to be a brief lull in the storm.

Micah knew without even turning toward the hallway that Gracie must have come into the room because Lilly's eyes had narrowed and her hands were now bracketing her slender hips. "You get your happy self right on in here, Gracie. Boy oh boy, my two husbands have been preaching to me for years that I should be thanking my lucky stars that the good Lord gave me boys. Because boys are so much easier to raise, they said. Girls are more emotionally driven, they don't think things through logically, they said. Well...I scoffed at that and now I'm dealing with a hell on wheels daughter-in-law that I had to practically hand deliver to my sons and then I had to talk her into staying with them when they screwed everything up right out of the gate. And tonight...oh don't even get me started on the train wreck I just walked in to up there."

Micah watched as Gracie's eyes never left Lilly's face. Lilly started pacing and he had to suppress a grin when he saw Dean and Dell both lean comfortably against a back wall, arms crossed over their chests, and indulgent half smiles curving their lips. They were obviously just going to let their lovely wife get it all out of her system before adding their two cents.

Trying to hold back his smile at the stunned expression on Gracie's face, Micah settled back and studied her as she focused on Lilly. From their previous conversations, Micah knew that Gracie considered her mother to be a strong-willed woman and had even compared her to Lilly a couple of times, so it made sense that Mama West had garnered her full attention. He sent up a silent prayer thanking the Fates for the gift of Lilly West, because it appeared as though she might be the one person among them that had a chance to reach Gracie.

GRACIE WATCHED LILLY West pace the room in the tallest, narrowest stiletto heels she'd ever seen on a pair of boots. The woman's balance was something to behold as she moved with fluid grace around the room, managing the oak flooring and throw rugs with equal ease. Her pencil skirt was so tight Gracie wondered how the woman got in and out of a vehicle, but when she let her gaze move to Dean and Dell, their lust-filled expressions spoke volumes. Gracie didn't doubt they were more than happy to lift their live-wire wife into any vehicle they could.

"Gracie, you better listen to me, young lady. These men are the best at what they do. They don't think I know about their jobs or the types of things they did in the SEALs, but they're wrong. I may not know all of it, but I know enough to know you are safer here than anywhere else."

Gracie didn't think Lilly had even looked at her so she was surprised at her next words. "I can tell what you're thinking, and if you think leaving will protect them, then you better yank that very pretty head of yours out of your ass. Because these are men of integrity and they'll follow you. And then you'll have all of your asses swinging in the breeze. And don't give me that little speech about painting a nice large target on everybody here, either. You think that asshat that is after you is going to just turn tail and chase you…that he isn't royally pissed off that somebody old enough to be his mother took out two of his hired guns? You think he isn't a bit miffed that he now looks like a boob to all his other criminal buddies?"

Micah and Jax had both tried to cover their snorts of laughter with feigned coughing fits, but Gracie hadn't been fooled. And when she saw Dean glance at his watch and shake his head as he handed a fistful of cash to his grinning brother, she wondered what the wager had been. Tobi had told her once that Kent and Kyle's dads regularly bet on various things related to their wife. Gracie could only assume they'd bet on how long it would take Lilly to make Micah and Jax lose their famous control.

When Gracie's attention flicked back to Lilly, she noted the woman had stopped not far from her and watched her intently. "Do you have any idea how lucky you are to have the resources of Prairie Winds at your fingertips? And I want you to think about how unhappy you are going to be when you find yourself stuck in some horrible hidey-hole all alone…knowing you are probably only a half a step ahead of that Baldballs asshat or whatever his name is." This time it was Gracie who snorted a laugh that was really more of a sob.

Lilly moved forward and grabbed Gracie's shoulders. "You are staying right here, Gracie. I didn't blow up those guys and their snazzy speedboat so you could just waltz out of here like a martyred princess. You'll stay right here and fight for what you want. I can see it in your eyes when you look at Micah and Jax. We can all see it. You've run long enough. It's time to stand and fight, sweetheart."

For the first time in years Gracie felt the dam inside her burst wide open with emotion and she'd just barely caught a glinting thread of hope as all the swirling feelings crashed around her. When Lilly opened her arms, Gracie didn't hesitate, she walked straight into a hug that felt a lot like her own mother's arms.

Chapter Twenty

JAX WALKED THE Wests out to their truck while Micah rocked Gracie gently as she slept curled up in his lap. She'd cried in Lilly's arms until she'd been swaying on her feet and Micah had stepped in and scooped her up and wrapped her in a soft quilt before setting with her in the rocker Micah's mother had given them. Within minutes she'd quieted and fallen into an exhausted sleep. As they neared the end of the porch he turned to Lilly, "I don't know how to thank you. We'd all tried and she wouldn't listen to reason."

Lilly smiled and touched his face tenderly, "You see, that was your mistake, sweetheart. You gave her a choice. She is frightened. Gracie loves you both and the thought of you being hurt is even more frightening than facing the man she knows will never let her escape again. She has a job she loves and hopes for a future that I'm willing to bet she'd probably given up on a long time ago. She is part of a close-knit group of friends that have become a second family to her and this is where her heart lies, so the thought of losing all of that terrifies her. Gracie didn't want to go, but she felt like it was a choice she had to make. I simply took away her choice."

Dean stepped forward and nodded to his brother who led Lilly to the truck and lifted her into the passenger seat before securing her seatbelt. When Dean turned his attention back to Jax his eyes were still filled with tenderness for the woman who obviously owned his heart. "Jax, remember the strongest women will make you earn their submission every step of the way. You and Micah are going to have to prove that you are worthy or Gracie won't ever feel like you will be strong enough to handle her and the baggage she is carrying. Being a Dom isn't all about controlling and cherishing...the real power is in bringing out the best in your submissive. Expecting their best and helping them get there. She needs to know that you expect her to grow and learn something new each and every day. Because every step she takes in that direction, will be a step closer to you."

Jax was grateful the elder West had pulled him into a quick embrace because it had given him just enough time to blink back the tears that had threatened to fall. When he pulled back he smiled down at the man who was nearly a foot shorter but much larger in wisdom and life experiences. "Thank you. I can't tell you how grateful we are for your help. And I want you to know your guidance hasn't fallen on deaf ears. It's easy to see why your sons are such men of integrity, sir."

After their guests had driven away, Jax took a few moments to collect his thought. While he waited for his nerves to settle, he sent off a text to Elza inquiring about Jen. After sending the message, he sent out a quick group message to several teammates asking their locations and if anyone was in the vicinity of western Costa Rica. The way his internal alarms were clanging it seemed prudent to get ahead of the game a bit by finding out where everyone was at the moment. Perhaps someone would be close enough to do a bit of snooping on Baldamino.

Walking back into the bedroom, Jax could hear the

shower running and Micah talking to Gracie. It was obvious she was not completely awake yet and he smiled as Micah seemed to be trying to hurry her along. "Gracie, come on, honey, help me out here. Step out of your jeans or I swear I'm going to cut you out of them."

"No. Too expensive. Sleep now. Shower later." Her sleepy voice was so airy-soft and sweet, and she sounded like a petulant child who was being denied their favorite toy.

Jax stepped around the corner just in time to catch her as she stumbled back into his arms. Micah was kneeling by her feet and took advantage of Jax's hold on her to finish undressing her. Smiling as Micah quickly undressed, Jax spoke softly against her ear, "I think I know just the thing to help revive our sweet sub. Why don't you get her into the shower and I'll be right back."

Returning quickly, Jax set the small cup aside and stripped in record time. Stepping into the shower, he pressed his foot between Gracie's dainty feet forcing her to widen her stance. Mouthing the words *hold her* to Micah, he picked up two small cubes of ice and quickly slid them up into her pussy and held them there as she came awake shrieking, "Holy shit on a Shetland pony. You stuck ice up my who-ha." She was dancing on her tiptoes and he grinned because there wasn't any doubt about the fact she was wide-awake now.

"I did. And do you know why?" He'd let his voice go deeper and when he felt her shudder in his arms, he knew the effort hadn't been wasted. She shook her head and he gave her lush ass a stinging swat. "You've been told several times to use words, *Cariña*, and it is well past time for gentle reminders."

"No…no, I don't know why you would stick ice cubes

in my pussy….Sir." She'd obviously added the title as a matter of attitude rather than in respect, so he struck the other cheek with an even sharper swat. "Hey. I said sir and everything, why did you spank me again?"

"Watch your tone or I'll keep giving you swats until you figure out the game has changed, *Cariña*." Looking up into Micah's face, Jax noted the satisfaction in his eyes. This was the part of D/s relationships that Micah always seemed to instinctively understand on a soul deep level. Jax didn't doubt for a moment that Micah would be pleased to be moving back onto familiar ground. Jax didn't soften his tone when he continued, "You're frightened and you need our Dominance to feel safe, don't you, *Cariña*? You're going to stay right here at Prairie Winds and do exactly as we tell you so we can take care of Baldamino."

Micah had moved close and pinched her nipples between his thumbs and forefingers before rolling them back and forth into tight peaks. "You belong to us, baby. Every squeal of joy, every tear of sorrow, every moan of pleasure, and especially every shudder of fear. It's all ours. And you won't deny us any of it, do you understand? Let's be sure you have a clear understanding, because this is the last time we're going to explain this to you. The next time we'll just take you to the club, tie you to a St. Andrew's cross in the main lounge, and send you so far into subspace you'll need to hitchhike home on the goddamned Space Shuttle. Now let's get your shower done so we can get you into bed. And if you're a really good girl, we might let you out from between us in a week or so."

Jax could see her reflection in the glass windows that made up one wall of the shower, and he wanted to smile at her confusion. He leaned down and bit the tender place where her shoulder joined her neck, and then licked at the light pink mark he'd left behind. He enjoyed the slight shudder that he felt move through her, and that little bit of quaking spoke volumes about how right Lilly West had been. *That's right, sweetness the game has changed.*

GRACIE WASN'T SURE what had happened but there had definitely been a change in the winds of their relationship that was for sure. Thinking back over what had happened today, nothing stood out as the cause of this sudden shift, so she could only assume it was something that happened after she'd fallen asleep. She wasn't entirely sure she appreciated their high-handed treatment, but then again there was something freeing about not having decisions to make. She'd been forced to make so many difficult choices in her life and there had been many times that she'd wished for someone in life that she could trust implicitly…someone she could just let handle things, even if it was only for a short time.

This was her chance to have that freedom, and now she was waffling on the edge afraid to take the leap of faith it would require. Was she brave enough? Could she let someone else step in? Let them deal with the man who had terrorized her dreams for more than a decade? The idea was as appealing as it was appalling. When she finally opened her mouth to speak, the words just didn't seem to make their way out. Looking up into Micah's eyes, she didn't see the frustration that had clouded them earlier in Kyle and Kent's office. All she saw now was a burning need to protect laced with a generous sprinkling of barely leashed lust.

Gracie also saw a flash of vulnerability in Micah's eyes

that was so fleeting and it was gone so quickly she wondered if she'd imagined it. But it was like a puzzle piece that fit too perfectly with everything else she knew about him, and that gave her the confidence that she'd been right. Micah Drake might be all confidence and swagger on the outside, but on the inside, he was still just a man who wanted and needed to be loved—even if he liked it spiked with a heavy dose of kink.

She'd originally thought Micah was the stricter of the two Doms, but she was beginning to understand they were equally dominant, and the ease with which they seemed to reverse their roles often had her losing track of who was playing "good cop" as opposed to "bad cop." The first time she'd heard Tobi apply the good cop—bad cop expression to her husbands, Gracie hadn't understood all the implications. But after spending time with Jax and Micah, she could see how apropos the analogy really was.

While she had been lost in thought, the men had washed and conditioned her hair before washing every square inch of her body. Her skin literally tingled with the increased sensitivity their touches had wrought. In the back of her mind, Gracie registered the fact the touches were soft but they'd steadily lured her into a very specific state of mind. It was only after they'd patted her dry with a warm towel and Jax had started combing her long hair that she realized she'd been operating on autopilot. *Damn my distracted self.* Her mother had often warned her that she was going to miss some important moments in her life if she didn't wake up and pay attention. Suddenly those words seemed much too prophetic and she hated the fact she'd missed the tenderness of Micah and Jax's hands moving over her body with such intimacy.

Vowing to stay in the moment, she turned to face

them both and smiled. "I...well, I'm sorry." She'd stumbled over the words despite the fact they'd been spoken from her heart, and she could see by their expressions she'd surprised them both. "I know I've been difficult about this whole thing, but the thought of anyone being hurt because of me...well, it just derails me, you know? But most of all I'm sorry for not treating you better. You both deserve so much more than I've given you. You've been so patient and kind. And I've held you at arm's length even when I said I'd *try*."

Gracie shifted her focus between Jax and Micah noting both men seemed to be studying her with an intensity bordering on predatory. When she stilled, their intent suddenly took on a fervor, it was almost a pulsing energy filling the room. She tried to hold completely still, much like a rabbit who'd caught the attention of the west Texas coyotes she'd read about. She felt herself shudder and knew they hadn't missed her body's reaction when she heard the rumbling growls deep in both of their throats as they converged on her.

The looks in their eyes was identical. Both men were intensely focused on her and lust fueled gazes were locked on her with single-minded intent. But there was also an underlying look of love and respect that was unmistakable, and that was what she'd always known was missing from Raphael's eyes. Even as a young and inexperienced girl, Gracie had recognized her captor's barely leashed raging sexual desire. She'd also known something was missing, too, even though she hadn't been mature enough to know exactly what it was. Remembering the last time she'd spoken with her captor, she could still see his eyes filled with possession rather than any regard for her as a person.

She took a deep breath and reminded herself that she'd

waited her entire life to see a man look at her the way Jax and Micah were in this moment, and she wasn't about to challenge fate by shying away now.

Chapter Twenty-One

Micah wasn't sure Gracie understood the significance of her words, but she had just given them a full-on green light and it was a pass he and Jax fully intended to use. Her admission to them that she'd agreed to try had been a stretch because she'd actually only admitted it to Tobi and Lilly, but he wasn't about to argue semantics with her. If she was willing to put herself in their hands, they would move heaven and earth to make sure she never had a moment of doubt that she'd made the right decision. He knew it would be a delicate balance to gain her trust and submission without damaging the fiery spirit residing within, but the reward would be a life spent loving a woman unlike any other they'd ever encountered.

He wrapped his hands around her wrists running his thumbs in small circles over her pulse points. "You are so responsive. Even the slightest hint of restraint sends your pulse racing. That is a huge turn on, love." She'd responded the same way the first night they'd met when he'd caught her delicate wrist as she'd shaken her finger at him. Smiling to himself at the memory, he enjoyed the slight hitch in her breathing as he tightened his grip just a bit. "I can't wait to see you with soft rope wrapped around your amazing breasts. They'll swell ever so perfectly as they lift up, seeking our touch and attention. We'll tie a clit knot that will be strategically placed—it will tease your body into a state of wanton need that only Jax and I will be able to satisfy by sliding into your sweet heat." *Oh yeah, I have your attention now, don't I, baby? Your imagination is taking you right to that moment.*

The first moments of a submissive's full surrender were the sweetest because she was making a conscious choice. The BDSM play that he enjoyed the most was ninety percent mental. Oh sure, Micah loved all the physical perks of fucking a beautiful woman into oblivion, but knowing he'd earned her trust was where the power was. The intimacy that was created between people when one essentially said, "I trust you with my body and soul. I know you only have my best interests at heart and that you'll always catch me, so it's safe to fall," that was the draw for both he and Jax.

He watched Gracie's dark eyes widen and heard her soft moan of need as Jax's hands slipped around her hips, pulling her back flush against him. Micah could see the understanding in her face as she let them step through the first line of barriers she'd built around her heart. He'd heard subs describe the feeling as willingly tumbling over the edge…knowing they could have pulled themselves back, but not wanting to. Seeing all of it working its way through her mind was like watching lightning during a summer thunderstorm. The light of understanding was a brilliant flash and it was followed by the rumble of the soul being shaken to its foundation.

Micah understood the power of what many Doms referred to as the "mind-fuck". But neither he nor Jax had ever been interested in playing those games. To them, the purity of a woman's trust was something to cherish. And even though they'd never found a woman they'd wanted to claim as their own before Gracie, they had still always respected the gift of her trust. Seeing Gracie's eyes become half-lidded with arousal and knowing that her responses were pure and genuine…that was the true essence of the power exchange of Dominant/submissive interaction. Every scene he and Jax had ever done was a rehearsal for this woman.

Sliding his hands up to cradle her head, he tilted her face until they perfectly aligned and he pressed his lips against hers in a kiss so fiery he was surprised they didn't both go up in flames. Gracie's lips were satiny smooth and already plump enough to feel like warm, moist pillows. Knowing that they'd be swollen from his efforts spiked his need even higher as he slid his tongue along the seam of her lips and heard her soft sigh as she opened herself to him. The heat of her mouth was amazing and the sweet hint of cinnamon that greeted him was an additional sensual treat.

The woman kissed like she was a born seductress. The way her body molded into his was threatening to shatter the last thread of his control. Pulling back from the kiss was sweet torture, but tonight was about finally fully taking control of her pleasure and Micah wasn't going to be denied the joy of taking his time, relishing her pleasure. He'd studied the tantric teachings of intimacy through touch and he intended to begin her introduction to those principals starting right now. Moving his hand up until it encircled her throat, he applied just the tiniest bit of pressure as he caressed the sides with just a fractional bit more pressure from his fingertips. When her eyes opened in surprise he saw the curiosity in them. *That's my girl. Focus everything you are—on what you feel in this moment. Nothing else exists right now but the three of us. Let yourself go. Lose yourself in us, baby.*

"Breathe with me, Grace. Deep breaths. Let the oxygen feed your soul and nourish your body as it prepares itself for everything Jax and I can give you." He knew his touch helped her focus on the words and he wanted to do a fist pump when her breathing immediately synced with his. Leading her through several deep breaths, he watched as her pupils became more dilated but her concentration was sharp and zeroed in on what she was feeling.

Every Special Ops soldier knows the effects of isometrics and isochronics on concentration and focus, so Micah knew the increased oxygen alone would help her mind and body work together, enhancing her pleasure. At this stage in a submissive's training, Doms had to begin pushing their sub to understand more about the vastness of the pleasures they could find in total submission. "Is your skin tingling, baby?"

"How did you know?" Her eyes had gone impossibly wide and she seemed so genuinely shocked that he'd known what she was experiencing that he couldn't hold back his smile.

"There are a lot of reasons for that to happen, but those are topics for another day. Right now, Jax and I are more interested in how your focus is being centered on your body's needs. If you'll put yourself in our hands, we'll take you to the heights you've been reading about in the novels you've enjoyed." He gave her mind a few seconds to absorb what he'd said before continuing. She'd quickly see some of the same principles in tantric sex as what she had been learning during the yoga training Tobi had been doing with her.

While Micah had been talking to her, Jax had been applying gentle pressure to various energy pulse points and they had both been noting her responses. Seeing her relax into a touch or flinch from it, told them a lot about what would enhance her sexual pleasure and what would pull her back from the edge. Learning all of her responses would make things better for all of them.

GRACIE TRIED TO will her mind into silence, but it didn't seem to be working. Micah and Jax's touches were lighting her up with sensation, but there seemed to be a part of her that just couldn't let go. Micah's lips pressed against her ear and then he spoke, "You're thinking again, love. We *will* get you out of your head, one way or another. I think that you have just had to be on guard for so many years that you've forgotten how to just let go. Am I right?"

"Y-yes, that is exactly right." She knew her words had been airy and soft, but his answering growl assured her Micah hadn't missed them.

Jax leaned over her and whispered softly against the opposite ear, "We'll get you there, *Cariña*, don't worry. It's going to be our pleasure to teach you about the freedom you'll find in submission."

Micah was holding her face in his cupped hands with his thumbs brushing softly against her kiss-swollen lips. "Have you noticed how much happier Tobi seems now?" When she nodded, he continued, "A large part of that is the fact she is secure in her Masters' love. She knows that no matter what happens, they will have her back. She'll never fall so hard or fast that they won't be there to catch her." Gracie had never considered Tobi's happiness was anything other than mind-blowing sex, but now had to admit Micah's theory was probably much more likely.

Jax gave her ass a firm swat, "*Cariña*, stop analyzing

everything and just feel. We're going to push you, more than you'll be expecting so I want to remind you of the stoplight system for safe words. We'll be checking in with you periodically, but I want to remind you that it is your obligation to tell us if you are frightened or getting near the end of what you can take. You've been given the word yellow for a reason. Don't hesitate to use it if you need to."

"Y-yes, Sir." Feeling her entire body tremble between them, she was grateful Jax had picked her up and moved her to the bed, even though she'd been surprised when he'd set her feet down on the soft throw rug to the side of the large bed rather than laying her on top.

"Bend over the edge of the bed and spread your feet apart. We're going to help silence your mind, love." She felt Micah's hand press gently, but firmly, between her shoulder blades. When her warm nipples touched the cool sheets she hissed and instinctively tried to stand back up, but his palm kept her flat. Before she'd even had a chance to fully register the cold she felt a stinging swat to her left ass cheek. "Don't worry, love, you won't be cold for long, I promise you."

Before he'd even finished speaking she felt the heat of his palm again, but this time he'd spanked her on the other side. Even though she'd flinched from the pain, it hadn't hurt as much as surprised her. But the quick bite shifted so quickly into a warmth that spread to her pussy, it was almost startling. She felt her pussy flood with moisture and she realized she'd unconsciously moved her legs back together. The next swat was stronger and then Micah leaned over her and asked, "Why did you move, love?"

Oh God, I don't want to 'fess up to this, damn! They will think I have no control at all. Hell, they'll probably pack me up and move me themselves. She heard Micah's growl of frustration just before he landed four more heavy-handed swats to her now pulsing backside. "As much as I love seeing my handprint on your luscious ass, I would much prefer to keep this an erotic spanking, love. Answer the question, don't edit your response. Your job is to simply answer immediately and with complete honesty. You will never be punished for being honest when we've asked you about your thoughts or feelings. You will, however, be punished for lying. And make no mistake, love, editing is lying."

"Umm, okay. Well, I was embarrassed because...well, my pussy got really wet and I...oh damn it all to donuts. I was afraid you'd be really turned off if my arousal started running down the inside of my leg." Even she'd been able to hear the tremble in her voice so there was no doubt both men had heard it as well.

Micah swatted her twice as Jax leaned down and kissed her cheek. *"Cariña,* that's where you are one hundred percent wrong and this is why we have insisted you be completely candid with us. Because misunderstandings like this will mushroom and drive a wedge between us. I think you'll agree that isn't what any of us want. What you need to know is that seeing your honey in shiny rivulets down your silky thighs tells us you are responding to what we're doing. It's a measure of how well we're doing our job and a huge turn on." Gracie let out a sigh as the reality of Jax's words settled into her soul. That little bit of information had a profound effect on her ability to relax.

Jax stopped and rubbed his hands over her ass cheeks in loving caresses that held the heat into her skin giving her a whole new round of arousal. "Your skin turns the most amazing rose color. It's hot beneath my hands and I can smell your sweet cream. It's like a siren's call to a Dom, love." Gracie felt his fingers slipping through her folds and each time he grazed them over her clit she moaned into the mattress. Feeling her mind starting to float away from her body was the oddest thing ever, but somehow she knew she was chasing something that was going to blind her with pleasure so she just let herself go.

Chapter Twenty-Two

JEN WALKED ALONG the beach with her sandals dangling from her fingers enjoying the afternoon sun's warmth atop her shoulders. The waves teased her relentlessly in their attempts to wash over her cotton candy pink painted toes. She'd been lost in her thought as she considered her plans for her last two weeks in Costa Rica when she heard the unmistakable sound of scooters coming up behind her. Glancing over her shoulder, she spotted two men much too large to be riding the tiny motorcycles as they gunned the small engines, spinning what Texan's referred to as "cat's asses" and sending huge arches of sand over one another.

Shaking her head at their antics, she couldn't help watching as the two boys in men's bodies whooped and hollered as they entertained everyone on the beach. Even from this distance it was easy to see they were brothers. Both looked to be well over six feet tall with dark hair, but it was their body language that was the most telling. Jen had just finished her studies in linguistics and applied communication, but it was her emphasis on non-verbal communication that was often the most valuable. Well…it was valuable when she wasn't too lost in her own thoughts to pay attention to what was happening around her.

Even though watching them had slowed her progress down the beach, the two men on the scooters hadn't seemed to "catch up" with her and she wondered briefly who they were performing for. She scanned the beach and saw the attention of every woman on the beach was focused on them so there was no telling who they'd set eyes on. She shook her head and couldn't hold back her laughter. They were so obviously having a great time their joy was contagious.

Both men were sporting haircuts similar to what Elza's brother, Jax, always had every time he'd been home on leave, so Jen wondered if they weren't perhaps American soldiers enjoying a few days downtime to blow off steam. Even though she could hear their laughter she couldn't make out what they were saying, but she was willing to bet that it was the same trash talking banter she'd heard Jax and his friends exchange at the McDonald's Austin mansion.

Since the men didn't appear to be moving her way, Jen turned and headed up the bank toward the sidewalk that would lead her back to the hotel she'd called home for the past few weeks. Concerned that she suddenly seemed to be attracting a lot of attention, Jen started to slip her sandals back off again in case she needed to run when a woman approached her and asked her name. The bluntness of the woman's question caused Jen to stutter and she barely caught herself before she blurted out her entire name. The elderly woman must have noticed her reluctance to answer because the older woman's expression softened. She amended her question inquiring if Jen was the young American woman who had gone missing, concerned that she might be in need of help. *What the hell?*

It had seemed to take forever to make her way back to the hotel because she'd been stopped so many times by well-meaning strangers offering to escort her to the authorities. The mile long jaunt had become a blur of stares and personal questions that often bordered on inappropriate. One thing Jen did notice was the fact she seemed to be seeing a couple of the same faces time and again. Two men dressed in dark suits seemed to be locals and were staying parallel with her on the other side of the street and she could hear the scooters from the beach about a half a block behind her. Deciding it was time to find out what was going on, Jen picked up her pace and was nearly running by the time she reached the hotel's enormous lobby. The smooth marble was cool beneath her bare feet and the change was just enough to jar her thoughts back in to line. She needed to find out what was going on. Information was always power and right now it seemed as if everybody had gotten a memo she'd missed.

Jen squinted at her phone's screen trying to read the new reports from U.S. news agencies before the hotel's Wi-Fi had booted her again. Damn but their internet connection sucked on its best days and today certainly wasn't one of those. She hadn't been aware of the young woman's disappearance until all those well-meaning strangers stopped on the street this afternoon. It had been obvious from their various accents most of them had been Americans worried about the fellow citizen who seemed to have just vanished into thin air.

When her phone had finally connected again, she saw her various inboxes full of messages. Jen had started wandering all around the hotel trying to find a strong enough signal to maintain the web connection she'd need to find out what the hell was going on. When she read the panicked texts from Elza and Jax, she planned to send them both messages assuring them she was fine and safely out of harm's way sitting in the hotel's inner courtyard as soon as she got a handle on what was going on.

Once she'd finally settled at the edge of the hotel bar and begun reading the sketchy reports, the hair on the back of her neck stood up and she had the most eerie feeling that she was being watched. Jen wasn't by nature paranoid, but the chill that raced up her spine when she'd spotted the men watching her had since turned her blood to ice.

It was easy to see why Jen had attracted so much attention from passersby, the pictures of missing student, Danielle Brandt, sent a new wave of chills through her. *Holy fucking hell, she looks enough like me to be my twin.* The fact the woman had been staying at the same hotel as her, only added to the strange feeling of foreboding Jen was feeling. Shaking her head in wonder, it was easy to see why she'd been stopped twice just walking through hotel's large lobby.

Jen fired off a text to Elza assuring her sweet friend that she was fine and assuring her she wouldn't hesitate to contact Elza's older brother, Jax, if she needed anything. She smiled when her phone vibrated in her hand almost immediately. Jen wasn't surprised to see Jax's number on the screen and even though she was tempted to let his call go to voice mail since she was in a public place, she didn't doubt for a minute he'd dispatch people to reel her in if he didn't hear for himself that she was safe.

"Hi, Jax, what's up?" Jen tried to keep her voice light because if Jax got even the faintest whiff of her fear there would be no containing his imagination.

"Where are you?" Typical Jax, cut right to the chase.

"Well, I'm fine, Jax. Thanks for asking. Oh yes indeed, Costa Rica is lovely this time of year. You really should make an effort to visit. And the accommodations are—" His growl cut her off and she knew she was pushing him, but old habits die-hard. She'd always liked Elza's older brother, but damn she'd just told him where she was in her text message.

Not long after she'd been hired as a "peer helper" for Elza, the McDonald family discovered she didn't have a family of her own and they'd quickly "adopted" her as their own. Her job assignment had been simple, she was supposed to help Elza adjust to college life. Smiling to herself, Jen thought back on how that single semester work-study gig had managed to stretch to a full five years at the McDonalds' insistence. Because Elza was profoundly deaf, she couldn't make out her brother's snarky tone, so Jen had considered it her *duty* to play the bratty younger sister anytime he'd attempted his high-handed big brother as guardian games.

Jax's frustration was easy to hear in his voice, "Knock it off, Jen, where are you? Right at this very minute, I want your *exact* location." Even by Jax's standards this was over the top. "Jen? I want an answer. Where are you? Stop stalling."

Damn, what crawled up his ass? I don't hear from him for months and all of the sudden he wants to go all macho-brother on me?

Glancing up, she noted that the two "suits" who had been standing across the bar's courtyard had moved to a table not far from where she was sitting. They seemed to be shifting in their seats as if they'd become uncomfortable that she'd noticed them. Of course the asshats were sitting in the Costa Rican sun dressed entirely in black, so it was possible they were just fighting off heat stroke. *Idiots.* But their continued sidelong glances in her direction made Jen think that probably wasn't entirely the problem. It certainly wasn't hard to see they were listening intently to her end of the conversation and she started mentally replaying everything she'd said wondering what might have made them so jumpy. When she looked at them pointedly, they quickly resumed their attempts to appear nonchalant. She didn't doubt their body language had been well rehearsed and was intended to make their prey feel at ease. She had a news flash for them…it wasn't working.

"I'm sitting at a small table at the edge of the hotel bar. The Wi-Fi signal is stronger here than in my room. Why? What's this about?" She and Jax had always been cordial, but he'd rarely phoned her. Most of their communication had been via either email or text messaging, but the urgency and annoyance were easy to hear in his voice.

"It's not something I want to discuss with you over the phone, but I'm sending a couple of friends to escort you back to Texas. They'll—"

"What? Hey, Jax, hold up for a minute." She didn't like interrupting him, but he really was going to have to explain what this was all about and give her some damned compelling reasons to cut her trip short, because she hadn't planned to leave until later this month. She still had two weeks of time off and she fully intended to enjoy it. "I am assuming this has to do with the other young woman who is missing. I can see why you'd be worried since she was staying at the same hotel and from what I can see in her pictures, we do resemble one another. And I really do appreciate that you are worried about me, but I'll be fine." Jen suddenly had a flash of herself talking to a brick wall and could only hope it hadn't been a moment of prophecy.

SAM MCCALL SLID onto one of the tall stools and set what

looked like a small gym bag in front of him. His younger brother, Sage, had done the same just a few minutes earlier. The bags both held some of the most sensitive listening devices currently available. Sage had directed his toward the beautiful woman sitting across the small patio from them. Jennifer Keating was a looker that was for sure. But Jax had warned them to tread carefully. He'd said the little blonde might look like sugar and spice, but she was actually whip smart and well versed in various forms of self-defense. They'd both laughed until he'd told them Jax had mentioned that he'd helped train her himself.

Sam looked her way and smiled, she certainly didn't appear pleased with whomever she was speaking to on the phone. Sam cocked his eyebrow at Sage in question and listened as his brother gave him a quick run-down. Seemed their lovely target was arguing with none other than Jax himself. Jax was a former teammate and the man they were currently helping. *I could tell her how futile that is if she'd just ask me.* Shaking his head, Sam thought back on their time working alongside Jax, and couldn't hold back his grin. Jax might look like a big teddy bear and appear easy going, but the man had a will of pure tempered steel. If Jax had decided the little blonde hottie was going back to Texas, then she was definitely going to be heading that way, one way or another.

Sam directed his bag in a different direction and listened to the two asshats who had been following her since she'd left her hotel several hours earlier. They hadn't seemed to be an immediate threat so he and Sage had decided to just observe. Considering the fact everybody seemed to judiciously ignore two men who appeared to have dressed hoping for a part in the next Men in Black movie, Sam figured they were likely the hired muscle of whoever was the flavor of the month as the local kingpin. *Christ, don't these guys know they'd be at least a bit more effective if they tried to blend in? Not to mention they might stave off heat stroke.*

Jax's group text to the team had reached them as they'd been packing to leave Costa Rica last night and it had only taken them a couple of hours to secure the equipment they'd needed. Pressing the ear bud in, he listened as Heckle and Jeckle ordered their drinks and flirted with the barmaid. He was about to decide they weren't an issue when their attention returned to Jen. The more he heard, the more grateful Sam was he'd insisted their equipment "live feed" back to Micah because there wasn't any doubt these guys were responsible for the missing American student.

~

MICAH LISTENED TO the live feed from Costa Rica and was glad he'd decided to record it when the men who had been following Jen began discussing their boss's plans for the two young women. He'd immediately sent messages to both Kent and Kyle requesting their help in the control room. Micah knew Jen was safe as soon as Sam and Sage had reported in that they were *"eyes on with their target"*. What they hadn't known was just how close they'd come to being too late. One more day…hell a few more hours, would have made all the difference. And none of their team was foolish enough to tempt fate a second time—Jen was leaving Costa Rica no matter how hard she argued with Jax. But first, they needed to make sure someone got Danielle Brandt out of Raphael Baldamino's compound and safely back in her family's care. And Gracie's knowledge of the layout of the man's home and the grounds surrounding it were going to be invaluable to the rest of the team he knew was already headed that way. *Hang in there, Danielle, the Calvary is on its way.*

Chapter Twenty-Three

Jen listened as Jax detailed all the reasons he had already planned for her return to Texas, and silently fumed. Sure, his reasoning was sound. Hell, it was probably even logical, but that didn't mean it didn't piss her off to no end that he'd already made all the arrangements without so much as even asking her opinion. When she was finally able to squeeze in a word and made that observation, he'd directed her to check her phone's history for all the missed texts and calls. Deciding that she'd formulate a plan of escape before his SEAL pals showed up, she finally managed to get him off the phone by pleading a dead battery. Sighing to herself, she got up and moved back toward the lobby.

Her room was on the second floor so she took the stairs, the elevator was just too unreliable and creepy. The wide staircase curved gently and had a wide landing halfway up featuring a small seating area. It gave the lobby an old world feeling of days gone by when life was slower paced and a lot more formal. Not that the Costa Ricans ever seemed to be in a hurry or that formality seemed anything they were interested in, but she still appreciated the ambiance of the old hotel. Stepping into the hallway, she pulled her key from her front pocket just as she felt hands grasp her upper arms in a bruising grip that warned she'd made a huge error by not paying attention. *Crap on a cookie, Jax is going bitch about this forever.*

"*Señorita*, not a sound. Let's go." They'd all but picked her clear up off the floor so any attempt to run was out of the question.

"Who the hell do you think you are? I'm not going anywhere with you two ass clowns." Jen opened her mouth to scream just as everything seemed to explode all around her. Suddenly the hands that had been tightened around her upper arms loosened and fell away at the same time she heard thuds and grunts as the men dropped like stones. The first hands were quickly replaced by two others and even though the grip wasn't as punishing, she still found herself on her tiptoes.

"Let's go, darlin'. Give Sage your key. We'll give you three minutes to pack out." True to form, Jen stiffened at the man's audacity, but at the same time she was grateful for the help because this guy was definitely American. Her mind was so programmed to assess language that she'd known immediately he was not only a native Texan, but she'd likely be able to pinpoint his hometown within a hundred mile radius. *Definitely eastern Texas, my bet's on Houston.*

―――

SAM MCCALL FELT a surge of electricity race up his arm the instant his fingers had connected with Jen's softly tanned flesh. A quick glance to his right told him Sage had felt it too. He'd wanted to kick the asses of the two thugs who had followed her into the lobby and his anger had escalated when they'd followed her up the wide stairway. *And the little doll needs her ass paddled for not being more aware of her surroundings as well. Christ, it fucking terrifies me to think about what might have happened if we hadn't been here. Hell, we'd be looking for two women instead of one.*

Sage had slipped the key from between her clenched fingers as Sam had told her she'd have three minutes to pack up her things. *Distract and conquer.* The instant he noticed she'd kicked off her sandals, he growled knowing exactly what the tiny tigress was planning. And as if she'd known the perfect moment, she'd shoved her pointed elbow into his ribs, squirmed from Sage's grip, and sprinted up the hall. Sam caught her in four steps—two more than it should have taken, but she'd actually stunned him for an instant with her quick jab. Sam heard Sage's chuckle as he opened the door and headed into her room.

"Put me down you big oaf. God save me from gulf coast jockeys and SEALs." *What? How the hell did she know where I'm from? Three fucking sentences and she knows where I'm from? Damn.*

Sage was already talking on his phone when he carried the whirling dervish into the room. "Yeah, we've got her. Heckle and Jeckle tried a snatch and grab, but we were only a couple of steps behind them. We've given sweet cheeks three minutes to pack out and she's already wasted a good share of that hissin' and spittin' at me like a pissed off kitten." Sam laughed when Jen crossed her arms over her chest and started tapping her foot. *Oh doll, if you think we were kidding about the time deadline you best be thinkin' again and getting that curvy ass into motion.*

Sam leaned against the door of her room and watched as she tried to take the phone from Sage's hands. It took everything in him to keep from laughing at the sight of Miss Five Foot Nothing trying to snatch the phone from his brother. Sage was within an inch of his own six foot three inch frame so she really was fighting a losing battle. "I'll show you hissing and spitting, you Neanderthal crawdad cowboy. Give me that damned phone." Sam wasn't sure whether it had been her words or the dumbfounded look on Sage's face, but he lost the battle and burst out laughing.

GRACIE SAT IN the West brothers' office and listened to the men discuss the American student who had disappeared in Costa Rica and her heart sank. She wasn't naïve enough to believe Raphael hadn't expanded his business to human trafficking because it would have been a logical step for someone as warped as she knew he was. She hadn't been able to tell Micah and Jax everything she'd seen and heard while she'd been held at the Baldamino estate because her mind had blocked so many of the details for so long that her memory had seemed sketchy and she hadn't wanted to seem like a flake. But recently, her subconscious started bubbling with details and as she listened now, more pieces of the puzzle emerged and for a few minutes she worried she might actually be physically ill. One of the maids had described the parties Raphael held at various locations around the estate and the sexually deviant acts were certainly not consensual.

Thinking about Raphael setting up a sex club where she was certain the safe, sane, and consensual rule wouldn't be adhered to, sent shudders up Gracie's spine. She listened as Jax answered his phone, it was obvious he'd been expecting the call and she hoped his friends had found Elza's friend. Watching as his worry lines smoothed away and were replaced by a boyish grin, Gracie felt herself release a breath she hadn't even realized she'd been holding.

Micah leaned over and squeezed her hand, "Baby, I know Jax as well as I know myself and I can tell you that smile means Miss Jen isn't taking any shit from the guys we sent to escort her home. I can hardly wait to hear about it." Gracie had turned to him when he'd started speaking and the softness in his expression spoke volumes to her about how fond both men were of Jen. Just as she started to speak, his phone chirped in his pocket. "Drake," his one word answer had told Gracie that Micah had shifted to all business in the blink of an eye. "Hot damn. Yes, if she and her family want to come back on the McDonald's jet, have them call Jax so he can coordinate it. That's great news, thanks for calling." He'd paused and then his smile had gotten much more strained and Gracie felt her anxiety begin to accelerate again. "Okay. Yes, we appreciate the heads up. Better to know than to see it on CNN. Hey, I'm not going to lie to you, this doesn't break my heart and doubt anyone else will give a rat's ass either."

By the time Micah had stopped talking, Gracie was wringing her hands together. Once Jax had confirmed the McCall brothers had indeed made contact with Jen everyone in the room turned their attention to Micah.

Micah explained that Danielle Brandt had been found wandering along a back road a few miles from Baldamino's estate. She was dehydrated and obviously had been beaten, but she'd been able to escape and walk over the rocky road barefoot until she'd been found by a local minister. Everyone had cheered, but it hadn't been hard to see that Micah wasn't finished relaying what he'd heard.

Listening to Micah describe the little bit of information he'd been given about the fiery explosion over the Costa Rican rainforest that had claimed the life of Raphael Baldamino had felt surreal. Gracie couldn't seem to sort out all the emotions rushing through her mind simultaneously. A part of her felt guilty for the joy she felt knowing she was finally free of the man who had cast a shadow over her life for more than ten years, but the relief she felt for her family and friends' safety was nearly overwhelming.

The room erupted into shouts of congratulations, which quickly turned to planning and phone calls to arrange for the rescued young woman and her family to return to U.S. soil. Gracie found herself sitting on the sofa wrapped in Tobi's embrace as she cried tears of relief. Looking up into her friend's eyes, all she could say was, "I can't believe it's finally over. After all these years...I'm finally free."

Tobi pulled back and looked at her with a rare intensity before saying, "You've always been free, Gracie. You always had the power within you to feel that freedom, it has never depended on that asshat. And don't you dare forget that everything you've ever dreamed of is within your reach, and there are two men in this room that very much want to help you reach every one of your dreams."

Epilogue

Four months later

GRACIE LAY BACK in soaking up the warm sunshine sipping her drink and twirling the paper umbrella between her fingers as she watched Jax and Micah race jet skis just off the coast with their friends. Her men had been asked to participate in a ceremony honoring a fallen teammate and the three of them had taken a little extra time to unwind while they'd been in San Diego. Gracie had instantly fallen in love with southern California. It was the first time she'd been able to visit the waters of her beloved Pacific since she'd fled Costa Rica so long ago. It felt wonderful to bask in the gentle ocean breeze and relax in the salty familiarity surrounding the ocean.

The past few weeks had been a flurry of activity filled with wedding planners, fittings, questions about a thousand details Gracie just hadn't been able to manage to care about. She'd finally abandoned everything to Tobi, Lilly, and "the mothers", as they were quickly becoming known. Her own mother had quickly bonded with both Jax's and Micah's mothers, and watching her mom and brother blossom had been one of the biggest blessings to come out of the chaos surrounding her. Well, except for the two men she was slated to marry in less than a week.

Waving as the men zipped past her yet again, Gracie

couldn't believe how much her life had changed since the night of the fire in Tobi's apartment. She'd be moving into her own beautiful home this next week and their new home took her breath away every time she walked through the door. The remodeling of the building had been completed in record time and Gracie had gotten a fast lesson in how quickly money could speed things along. Lilly had helped coordinate that project as well and it had quickly become obvious why the men had allowed her to "help". It seemed no one was able to say "no" to Hurricane Lilly and stick to it. Gracie had watched in awe one afternoon as the woman had dealt with electricians, flooring specialists, and florists with the same iron-willed grace. The irony that Kyle and Kent West had married a woman so much like their mother hadn't been lost on Gracie.

She'd been so lost in her thoughts, she hadn't even noticed one of the nearby bar's servers standing beside her chair holding a tray. There was something about the young man's unease that had her sitting up straight. "I'm sorry to disturb you, Miss, but I've been tasked with delivering this to you. The gentleman who left it, declined to leave his name. He assured me you would know who it was from."

When he lowered the tray, Gracie felt all of the air leave her lungs. Her entire body began to tremble and she couldn't breathe. A single red rose lay diagonally across the tray…and it was the last thing she saw before everything faded to black.

The End

Books by Avery Gale

The Wolf Pack Series
Mated – Book One
Fated Magic – Book Two
Tempted by Darkness – Book Three

Masters of the Prairie Winds Club
Out of the Storm
Saving Grace
Jen's Journey
Bound Treasure
Punishing for Pleasure
Accidental Trifecta
Missionary Position

The ShadowDance Club
Katarina's Return – Book One
Jenna's Submission – Book Two
Rissa's Recovery – Book Three
Trace & Tori – Book Four
Reborn as Bree – Book Five
Red Clouds Dancing – Book Six
Perfect Picture – Book Seven

Club Isola

Capturing Callie – Book One

Healing Holly – Book Two

Claiming Abby – Book Three

I would love to hear from you!

Email:

avery.gale@ymail.com

Website:

www.averygalebooks.com/index.html

Facebook:

facebook.com/avery.gale.3

Instagram:

avery.gale

Twitter:

@avery_gale

Excerpt from Fated Magic

The Wolf Pack
Book Two
by Avery Gale

K IT PACED THE length of her husbands' office like a caged animal during the entire meeting regarding the boy her mother simply referred to as Braden. Jameson hadn't hesitated a moment in his agreement to take the teenager in and the rest of the meeting had been taken up with logistics and planning for his safety as well as the safety of everyone else living at the estate. Kit was in favor of taking him in and knew her friend well enough to know where he'd be staying once he arrived. It was obvious that Angie had felt a very real connection to the young man and Kit was relieved that everyone was rallying around him. Her restlessness had nothing to do with Braden...no her frustration was directed entirely at her two Alpha mates.

Trying to tell me that I have to wait for the next full moon to run. Damn wolves think they can rule the world just because they are the Alphas of the pack. Don't think so, fellas, I am running tonight if I have to leap out of a damned window naked and fly into the forest on a damned broom. She'd always detested the image of witches on brooms because it was about the most ridiculous bit of imagination in history if you asked Kit.

Brooms? Really? Like any self-respecting witch needed a damned broom.

Spending the past four months cooped up in the estate was taking a toll on her sanity and if she didn't get out soon she was going to be a loon. At first she'd been too busy with the babies to worry about the fact she often spent the entire day in her pajamas. But the only thing that had kept a lid on her growing frustration was the fact she'd been spending a lot of quality time in the gym expending copious amounts of energy in every sort of physical outlet she could find. Well, all but the one she wanted to be enjoying. Her husbands had, for some reason, decided vanilla sex was more acceptable for a "mother" and she was seriously considering drowning them both.

How can anyone who can be replaced by a battery-operated device consider himself the Lord and Master of his Kingdom? I didn't even get a honeymoon. Nope I went straight from caught to mated to knocked up. Once they got what they wanted all was well in the Wolf brothers little Alpha paradise. Whoever decided men should be the leaders of a pack or any other group really needed to study ancient history. Fat fairies will fly over Philly before I settle for vanilla sex for the rest of my life. It's just mean. Show me all the fun of kink and then take it away? I don't fucking think so.

She'd finally received the go-ahead from the doctors to shift and run tonight and then Jameson had "suggested" that she wait until the next full moon because of the meeting she was currently ignoring. Well she'd be showing them a thing or two in a couple of hours because she had already made arrangements for the twins to spend the night with a couple of their nannies and she planned to make an appearance in the forest come hell or spell.

Made in the USA
Columbia, SC
03 July 2017